TOO GOOD TO BE UNTRUE

BY

JOSEPH A. WAILES

OUTLAW PRESS
RAWHIDE, TEXAS

OUTLAW PRESS
2980 PHYLLIS LANE
RAWHIDE, TEXAS
75234-6425

THE WINNER OF THE HUMAN RACE

BY
JOSEPH A. WAILES

I_WHEN LIGHT BECAME A MAN

II_THE LONGEST NIGHT

III_ANCIENT DREAMS, NEWBORN VISIONS

IV_WAR OF THE BOOK

V_THE THIRD UNIVERSAL EVENT HORIZON

VI_HARVEST MOON

VII_TOO GOOD TO BE UNTRUE

BOOKS AVAILABLE AT OUTLAW PRESS

TABLE OF CONTENTS

0_FOREWORD............................7

1_THREE-FOLD LINES................9

2_ONE GOD, THREE KINGS, AND SEVEN GIFTS............................16

3_BEFORE THE BOOK WAS SEALED....................................25

4_JUST A COUPLE OF MINUTES...30

5_HOLY IS HIS NAME................38

6_DISTANT RELATIVES.............41

7_PRESSURE-COOKED..............52

8_THE VIEW FROM INSIDE THE UNIFIED FIELD........................61

9_MERCY WITH TEETH.............71

10_THE BOTTOMLESS PIT..........93

11_T MINUS 6........................125

12_SEVEN FLAMING SWORDS...130

13_THE VOICE OF A STRANGER.138

14_THE SEVENTH COMBAT MEDIUM................................143

15_THINKING IN 3D................160

16_WHEN THE MONSTER SNORES................................174

17_GOOD NEIGHBOR POLICY...190

18_FIRE AND BRIMSTONE.......199
19_BLESS THE MAN WHO BLESSED THE MOON...........................213
20_FOUR SHOTS LEFT............222
21_THE MYSTERY OF ELEVEN.236
22_BREAKING THE FANGS OF THE SERPENT..............................243
23_THE LAST TIME I MET GWEN...................................258
24_TWO SHARP EDGES...........270
25_THE MATTER OF GRAVITY..279
26_THE PLACE OF DARKNESS, AND THE HOUSE OF LIGHT............308
27_WAR COUNCIL..................334
28_ABOUT THE AUTHOR.........362
29_BACK-JACKET TEXT..........364

FOREWORD

This last volume concludes the seven-book set which began with "When Light Became A Man". When I was nearly finished with book 6, "Harvest Moon", I noticed that a pattern was already woven, unintended by me, right into the fabric of the seven-book set, even before I knew for sure that there would be a seventh book. Each of the books corresponds a lot to the themes of the seven gifts of the Holy Spirit.

Book 1 was much about prophecy, and book 2 was much about healing, and book 3 was much about teaching, and book 4 was much about preaching, and book 5 was much about giving, and book 6 was much about the principles concerning leadership (power and authority). I was not surprised when book 7 turned out to be much about mercy, as expected. Someone else installed that pattern in these books. I did not even know it was happening, until almost done writing all of them.

Of course, there is a wide spectrum of subjects in each book, encompassing most regions of Heaven, Earth, and Outer Space, and all of Time, and a look both forward and backward, into Eternity. It took 5 years of my own life to type it all down. I do believe that the dreams came from God, so please pray that I was right. I meant no offense to anyone. I just tried to write down the dreams I was shown.

THREE-FOLD LINES

In the Word of God, it is recorded that "a three-fold cord is not easily broken". Anyone that was ever a sea-going sailor (beyond some pleasure cruise) almost certainly spent some time learning about knots and lines, from 1/8 inch nylon cord, to 5 inch hawsers. Almost all modern lines consist of three primary strands. In Boy Scouts, we learned how to spin fibers into lines, but it is much faster and simpler to produce a two-fold line, instead of a three. The problem with that approach is that a two-fold cord wears out quickly, breaks under strain, and eventually proves that it is not worth the time to fabricate it. Once again, ancient, eternal wisdom from the Word of God proves that God knows best.

A strong parallel is observable in human relationships. While a couple may be very strong, a family is stronger. The incorporation of the third primary strand amplifies durability, exponentially.

In the Word of God, we are also instructed to present testimony, or witness, in the mouths of two or more witnesses, so that every word may be established. God has presented Himself unto us in three aspects. The first aspect is Father (Creator), the second aspect is Son of God, (Savior), and the third aspect is Holy Spirit of God (Comforter). It is worth noting that the original meaning of the word "comfort" is "with strength", or, in this case, "with Power and Authority".

Even though this is the order in which the good Lord revealed Himself unto us, His sequence for Salvation is entirely opposite. God informs us in His Word, that no man can come unto King Jesus Christ, unless God (as Holy Spirit) first draws the man to Him. The Word of God also informs us that no man can come to the Father, except through King Jesus.

We are "saved by grace, through faith". No man can even possibly have any faith, unless the Holy Spirit first convicts the man of sin, of righteousness, and of judgment. Of sin, because they do not believe in King Jesus, of righteousness, because Jesus went to the Father, and of judgment, because the ruler of this world is already judged.

We do not believe because we "chose to believe". We did NOT choose Him: He chose us! We believe only because God was gracious enough to allow each believer, whom He chose, to become a believer, in the first place.

The only part, where our free will is active, is whether or not we choose to obey! Just because a person believes, that does not automatically make them choose to obey. Our good Lord told us that if we do actually love Him, we will choose to obey. Otherwise, how would anyone dare to call Him "Lord", but not obey Him? If you love someone, you want them to be happy.

Another thing that bothered King Jesus was when people went through the motions of religious observances, but totally neglected "the weightier matters of the Law", which He then went on to list as Justice, Mercy, and Faith. We know from the historical evidence that Father (Creator) is the very Living Presence of perfect Justice. In ancient times, either you did right in the sight of the Lord, or He destroyed you. He still does that, today.

A second parallel is evident with King Jesus Christ being the very Living Presence of Mercy. Even framed, murdered, and dying upon the Cross, He asked the Father to grant forgiveness unto the human race, which was way too stupid to understand the magnitude of the horrible atrocity which they were still committing, as He spoke forgiveness unto them, while they were still murdering Him.

We have already noted and illustrated how the Holy Spirit is a continuation of the theme, as the very Living Presence of Faith. No man can believe without Him, and no one can continue to overcome with faith, unless the Holy Spirit gives the person strength of faith.

We can therefore conclude that our good Lord considers the "weightier matters of the Law" to be very weighty, indeed, because they directly correspond unto His three Holy Aspects. First is Justice, which MUST be fulfilled. Next proceeds Mercy, but only AFTER Justice is completed. When Justice and Mercy have been met, Faith can be granted, and God has promised that He will do that, since, as we are informed in Peter, our faith is what our good Lord is mining, as the chief treasure which He is going to produce in the human race, before His return!

In the 5th chapter, of 1st John, we are given a crystal clear picture of just how God has set up His Own Testimony, about Himself. Verses 7 and 8 read,

"For there are Three that bear record in Heaven, the Father, the Word, and the Holy Ghost: and these Three are One. And there are three that bear witness in Earth, the Spirit, and the water, and the blood: and these three agree in One."

Therefore, God has followed His Own instructions, and sent His Testimony in three forms of Witness, both in Heaven, and in Earth. I think we must, also, consider these things to be the "weightier matters of the Law", and remember to apply them, in our daily walk with King

Jesus, and in our long-term personal plans. God obviously wants us to get the point, and to accept it as Truth!

ONE GOD, THREE KINGS, AND SEVEN GIFTS

Almighty God, the Creator of all Reality, has been revealing His nature and character unto mankind in multiple ways, ever since He first said, "Be LIGHT!"

The Word of God tells us that God may be known by the astonishing aspects of His Creation. The Universe is vast, but God is larger! Time is old, but God is eternal! The Universe was created, and can be destroyed, but only, in either case, by God, Alone. God was never created, and can never be destroyed.

God ranges full-spectrum, from the ultra-sub-atomic, in areas too small for mankind to perceive, all the way to the ultra-macro super large scales, like super clusters of thousands of galaxies, and the entire Universe, known, and unknown to mankind, both. The Word of God declares that light and dark do not limit the Eyes of God, but that He sees everything that exists, in perfect clarity. "Neither is anything hidden from His sight, but all things are naked, in the Eyes of Him with Whom we have to deal!"

When it comes to our seeing Him, it is a different matter, entirely. The Word tells us that "No man can see God, and live." The Word also proclaims that "No one hath seen God at any time. The only Begotten Son, He hath declared Him." We are also informed that God dwells in unapproachable Light, and no man can come unto Him, except by King Jesus Christ.

King Jesus also answered Philip, "He that hath seen Me hath seen the Father. I and the Father are One!"

Remember that the Law of God requires that a matter be established in the mouths of two or more witnesses.

Almighty God, in His three aspects, as Father, Savior, and Holy Spirit, has generously given us a spectacular set of witnesses about His true Personality, and His mysterious inner nature, through (1) His Universe, (2) His Scripture (delivered through Holy Prophets, and proven by miracles, all through the centuries), (3) His Holy Begotten Son, King Jesus Christ, with unique miracles and His Own Resurrection, (4) the Presence of the Lord Holy Spirit inside each born-again follower of King Jesus Christ, and the changed, God-glorifying life that is made manifest in the life of the obedient believer, (5) the continuing modern-day fulfillment of ancient Scripture Prophecies, and the obvious precise correlation to current events and headlines, (6) even the very structure and function of the Seven Gifts of the Holy Spirit, and (7), the ultimate return of King Jesus Christ, in His resurrected Body, with all of the resurrected saints with Him, after the tribulation, and after the sun and moon go dark.

Item number (7) in the above list may catch your eye first, but that topic is explored in depth, in the preceding books, especially "The Longest Night", and "Ancient Dreams, Newborn Visions", and "Harvest Moon". For this discussion, let us instead focus upon item (6).

The seven gifts of the Holy Spirit are (1) Prophecy, (2) Healing, (3) Teaching, (4) Preaching, (5) Giving, (6) Power and Authority, and (7) Mercy.

A strange, newly revealed perspective on this matter shows that Gift (1), Prophecy, corresponds directly to the Father, since He was the first aspect to give a Prophecy, in Genesis.

There should be little debate that (2) Healing, directly corresponds unto King Jesus Christ. His healing miracles were one of His most convincing evidences of precisely the truth, that He is God, in the Flesh.

We do call King Jesus "Teacher", and He is, but, since He is currently awaiting the Father's launch order, for His Personal return, to the Earth, the Holy Spirit is presently the aspect of Almighty God which is working within us, as (3) "Teacher". The Word of God decrees "And they shall all be taught by God!" King Jesus illustrated this in point, when the Pharisees asked in amazement, "How does this Man know letters (meaning the Law of God), having never studied?"

King Jesus answered them that the doctrine (meaning knowledge) was not His, but from the One that sent Him.

So, we can perceive that Almighty God even reveals Himself, in the dimensions of His Holy Gifts. In all three aspects, He performs Prophecy, Healing, and Teaching.

When it comes to Gift (4), Preaching, it takes a Man to Preach. Even though Jesus told us that He only spoke the things that His Father said to speak, and did the things that His Father said to do, and it was the Holy Spirit that gave Him perfect, supernatural knowledge, it still took a Man to Preach.

In similar manner, we can notice that for Gift (5), Giving, it takes the Father to Give. We are told that "Every good and perfect gift comes down from the Father of Lights, in Whom there is no variableness, or shadow of turning." Also, King Jesus Christ told us to ask the Father, directly, for whatever we needed, and to trust that He already knew of our need, before we could even ask. He promised that we can ask, and receive, so that our joy may be full.

For Gift (6), Power and Authority, we know that King Jesus Christ has all Power and Authority, in Heaven, and in Earth. We also know that for this present age, here upon Earth, it is the Living Presence, of God, as the Holy Spirit, within the re-born, that enables us to believe, and to overcome temptation, by not entering into it. One way to put it might be, "Don't look, don't stumble." We are supposed to resist the devil, but flee from temptation, since only King Jesus could overcome the world (temptation). So, for now, the Holy Spirit is the source of Power and Authority within each believer. King Jesus is the trailblazer, the true pioneer, and explorer, and discoverer, and indeed, we do follow Him, but it is the Holy Spirit that is leading us home to King Jesus, changing us along the Way.

Finally, what about Gift (7)? Which aspect of Almighty God is most evidently manifesting His Presence, in the Gift of Mercy? Well, it truly appears to be the overlapped Presence of all Three: Father, Savior, and Holy Spirit. Mercy is the entire end-game objective of Almighty God, and the core strategy which the Father gave as a Prophecy, in Genesis. Remember that God warned all of

Creation not to interfere, as He proceeded to "make Man, in His Own image".

Please also recall that King Jesus Christ is also named "The Lamb that was slain, before the world began". God knew that mankind would fail, so He set forth Jesus, even before the world was made, to solve the sin problem, forever. King Jesus told Pilate that it was for this cause that He had come forth, "that I might bear witness to the truth".

King Jesus had also proclaimed that He had come to seek, and to save, that which was lost. In the end, King Jesus will execute Judgment upon all, and disburse life or death to those whom He will.

So, Almighty God reveals Himself in all seven Gifts, but it is His aspect as King Jesus that most fully manifests Mercy, and accomplished the Mission for which the Father sent Him. I never heard of anyone else that could pray forgiveness for their killers, even while they were still being murdered, to pay for the crimes of those same monsters!

BEFORE THE BOOK WAS SEALED

In the midst of infinite nothingness, and eternal emptiness, there was Something, and that Something was a Person, and that Person was Almighty God. Nothing else, and no one else, existed yet, since God had not yet created anything.

God was not tired, but He was deep in detailed thought, making Plans, and working out all the bugs that might arise, way before He even started His construction project. He was about to begin building a brand-new home, for Himself, and all of His Children, and none of them was even born, yet.

God Himself was blazing forth unapproachable Light, because that is Who He is: Living, Unapproachable Light!

The Light is purest, absolute white, with equal components of blue, corresponding to the Father, and red, corresponding to the Son, and green, corresponding to the Spirit. When the projective primaries are emitted in precisely equal intensity, from precisely the same emitter, the result is pure white light. God has always been fully God, and He has always been fully Father, and fully Savior (except waiting for the birth of His flesh body), and fully Spirit, as well. God was, is, and always will be all three aspects of Himself, simultaneously. No one else but God can be three distinct people, at the same time, and still only be just One God. It is not something that He does, it is the just the Way that He is.

When God had finished His initial planning stage, He first created the Book of Life, and in it He wrote all of the names of those which He chose, knowing before He created them what each person would be, and where they would live, and what their birthday, and death-day, was, in each person's case. God recorded all of those precise details, about every saved living person, even before making the world. He did not do that so that He would not forget any of us.

He did that so that it will forever stand as proof and testimony to the absolute precision of God's perfect knowledge, even unto things never yet made. He told us way back then, and wrote it down, so that when it comes to pass, we will forever believe.

He did that, and then locked the Book closed, with an absolutely unbreakable Seal. That Seal can only be opened one Time (and the Time is very specific), and then, only by King Jesus Christ, at the Time of the Great White Throne Judgment. (Anyone that wishes to dispute that truth is in direct disagreement of the Prophecy that King Jesus Christ dictated in Revelation.) Until the Great White Throne Judgment, the Seal cannot be broken, and nothing at all can either be added or taken out!

Almighty God does all kinds of wonders that no one else but Him can ever do. After all, He is God. His Ways are so far above us, and so vast and complicated, that we can never completely understand it all. We know that God can do anything. We know that He can make it last forever, or destroy every trace of it, forever. We know that He is the most serious subject any thinking creature might ever consider, and to fail to willingly obey Him is certain death. We know that God is very good, and we all should want to willingly obey Him, anyway.

At the moment that the Book was Sealed, King Jesus Christ had to agree, right then, to allow Himself to become "The Lamb That Was Slain, Before The World Began". Once the Savior had agreed with the Father, that such was the only Way, to achieve the objective of all

Creation, that Mankind would be made into God's image, then it was time for launch.

The Father looked with great love upon His Only Begotten Son, and said, "You are My Son! This Day, I have begotten You!"

As King Jesus Christ smiled with joy back at the Father, the Father said, "You are the True Light. Now, I send You forth. Go there, Light!"

Now the Light shines in the darkness, and the darkness cannot put it out, and the world is made by the Light. Now God has begun separating the Light from the darkness. The Light is destroying the darkness. Thank God!

JUST A COUPLE OF MINUTES, PLEASE

It's extremely easy for each of us to become very caught up in our own personal schedules and plans. In the 21st Century, anything that is not high-speed, high-definition, high-capacity, high-density, or high-dollar, is usually not considered to be even minimum threshold for usefulness.

People rush here and there, and then, rush frantically back there and here again! Most of us get so adapted to our frequently worn pathways that we just continue to carve deeper and deeper ruts into our lives.

It can be a real imposition, whenever someone or something else intrudes upon a person's schedule, and sometimes even a distraction for as little as two or three minutes can break one's rhythm, momentum, or train of thought. Even so, sometimes a deliberate break in the flow of "business as usual" can be a very beneficial thing.

About a century ago, a war began that threatened to destroy most of the civilized nations and societies of the world. People called it the "war to end all wars". New and astonishingly horrible weapons and delivery systems were invented, and there was a very real danger that mankind could be self-defeated back into a degenerated state, that might be the rough equivalent of several centuries of human progress and knowledge being lost and forgotten. People could have been driven back, past the Middle Ages, to the Dark Ages.

Thirty years after that, another, far deadlier war began, and this one had the bitter capacity to drive humanity all the way back to the Stone Ages. Since that time, many smaller, scattered conflicts have arisen, but nothing else global in scale, for the last seventy years.

The Cold War was a slow burning fuse, which most people think has been snuffed completely out. Instead, the tensions between East and West are more like the boiling magma dome of Yellowstone. It is all out of sight, underground, unseen, and unheard, but churning and seething with enormous explosive force, all bottled up, just waiting to erupt! It is already long overdue for explosion, it is just a matter of time, and all it needs is the trigger mechanism or event to release overwhelming destruction, on a global scale. Absolute annihilation of all life upon our planet is quite possible. This is, somewhat uniquely, a true statement for both the Yellowstone magma dome, and the East-West power struggle, for control of our planet. The cataclysmic events which might be produced are not compatible with life "as we know it".

In the cases of each of the previous major wars, and some of the minor ones, the conflict was won for the side of the "good guys", for want of a better term. (After all, the "bad guys" on the other sides always wanted to enslave, torture, rape, and murder people for no reason, except that the monsters loved to glorify the devil.)

There can be no real doubt that victory was done strictly by the grace and power of Almighty God, but He used a lot of humble, unselfish human soldiers to get the job accomplished. "Praise the Lord, and pass the ammunition!" was a battle slogan repeated very often during those savage wars. The enemy soldiers were well-armed, tough, and smart, also. The only way that our soldiers could win was to fight with fierce faith, trusting their futures, and their lives and deaths, to the Savior, in Whom they believed. They had to commit everything that they had, and everything that they were, and give it all willingly to God, willing to die and be buried in a strange land, far from home.

Now, it is certain that a person that is willing to risk it all like that, and do it to defend strangers back home, people that he never met, and never would, is a person that should be treated with some genuine respect. If a momentary interruption of a couple of minutes is bothersome, just try to imagine how bothersome it must be to have your entire life uprooted, and your entire future in uncertainty, and your life expectancy unknown (from a few more seconds, to many more years).

Today is Veterans' Day, 2011. For almost a century, people have been asked to stop, every single November 11th, at precisely 11:00 A.M., and to please observe two minutes of respectful silence. The purpose is to break that frantic rush and rhythm, and to cause people to stop and remember that those free and frantic lives and schedules are only possible because of all the noble men and women that humbly wore military uniforms, and obediently went many times into the teeth of death, and fought not just to escape their personal destruction, but to kill a deadly threat to their fellow Americans, no matter what the cost. The mission-required mindset is always the same: "Mission Accomplished", WHATEVER it takes!

This is precisely the mindset that King Jesus Christ wore upon His noble mind, like a true crown of glory, and it also served as a bullet-proof helmet. The lies and doubts of the devil could not invade the thoughts of King Jesus. As He said, the devil had nothing in Him. Something else to remember about King Jesus is that He is also the ultimate Undefeated Warrior of all time, and He still never has lost a single fight. His greatest fight He had to give His Own Life to win, but He still did not lose the battle.

It seems almost incidental that the victory of King Jesus entirely destroyed the power and authority of the devil, and ended the reign of terror, forever, since His greater struggle was not only to control Himself during His torture and death, but to even remain loving and tough enough to actually, sincerely pray forgiveness, for His Own murderers, as we were killing Him. No one else but King Jesus could ever have won a fight like that!

So, now taking it upon myself to speak for all the other honorably-discharged veterans, we would like to remind everyone (that is a U.S. citizen) that your personal freedom and security depends upon people like us. Even though we were willing to put it all on the line for you, we would at least like for your hearts to feel genuine thankfulness, and to show some sign of it, at least once a year, for at least two minutes.

From now on, whenever November 11th rolls around, wherever you are, at the precise hour of the stroke of 11:00 A.M., pull over the car, hang up the cell phone, mute the television, stop telling gossip, and stand silently for two minutes, remembering all of us, especially the ones that did not make it back home. If you are a Christian, we also ask that you say a prayer of thanks, and pray for us and our families, since we fought for yours. Whether you pray or not, at least stop, and remember, for just two little minutes. Is that really too much for us to ask of you?

Try to look at it this way. Even if you do not value us, or care at all about the sacrifices that we made for you, there is Someone which you most certainly should remember, and honor. Even if you forget to honor Him most of the year, try to remember the greatest Warrior that ever lived, or died, and at least spend the two minutes giving thanks for Him!

HOLY IS HIS NAME

The Word of God reveals in Ezekiel that the only reason that Almighty God is going to save anyone, except for Noah, Job, and Daniel, is not for our sakes, but for His Holy Name's sake. In ancient times, and still the case today, a person's name is linked with their character, their honor, and their fame, or their lack of those qualities. In Proverbs, it is recorded that "A good name is more to be chosen than great riches, and loving favor rather than silver and gold."

When a person's words match their deeds precisely, they are considered to have integrity. For Almighty God, Word and Deed are literally the two sides of the same coin. God has always had perfect integrity, and His Word, and Deed have always been exactly the same thing. For God, to speak is to act. God takes the certainty of His Word so seriously that

He even swore a solemn oath by His Own Life, saying, "As I live," says the Lord, "My Word shall not return unto Me void, but it shall accomplish My Purpose!"

Therefore, it is a very big deal unto the Lord to keep the promise which He made unto Abraham, to save the children of Israel, because He swore it by His Holy Name. He is not doing it for us, but for the integrity of His Name, His Word, and His Holy Spirit. He is called, by the angels, "HOLY! HOLY! HOLY!" Indeed, He is, was, and always will be Holy Father, Holy Savior, and Holy Spirit.

In a very real, if not often noticed, perspective, one might very well consider "Holy" to be God's first Name. Whether one is referring to Father, Savior, or Spirit, the first Name is still "Holy".

People might do well to remember that fact, and that when they casually say "Holy ..." the only possible acceptable second word in that phrase is "God"! Unless one can grasp and abide by the fact of reality that God, and only God, is to be called or considered "Holy", how can anyone claim to love Him, and then use His first Name in a shameful manner?

Wouldn't it be wonderful, if every time someone started to say the word "Holy" in vain, they instantly heard God's deep Voice answer, "Yeah, what do you want? I'm busy!" It probably would only take about one of those replies per lifetime to make people start watching what trash they carelessly spew out of their mouths, especially if they're taking about God's first Name!

DISTANT RELATIVES

Adam and Eve climbed carefully along the very top of the steep ridge line of rock, as they worked their way higher and higher into the upper elevations. They were moving into their winter cave, where the storms would not disturb their long winter naps, while they exercised, slept, ate, stayed warm, and waited out the cold, until they could emerge with the spring thaw. They had already stockpiled the cave with much dried fruit and vegetables, and many kinds of edible and delicious vegetarian fare that is not available in the modern world, since most of the finest plants have become extinct, from pollution. For the wolves, they even had a thing they called "carnivore tree", which had large, crunchy fruit, that tasted just like good raw meat, to a wolf, and even the branches of the tree tasted like juicy bones with rich marrow!

Wolf bounded ahead with She-wolf, as they scouted the path ahead, looking for any surprise dangers. Ever since the people had been evicted from the Garden, the wolves had made it their personal, life-long missions to always guard the humans that they loved, like their own lives, even with their own lives, if it came to that. Every few minutes, She-wolf would race back past them, cleanly slipping by, without more than the quick whisper of her fur lightly brushing by their legs, as she scanned the pathway behind them for anyone, or anything, trying to sneak up their blindside. Things had changed for everyone, since the Garden, and a relaxing stroll across the countryside was a fading memory, these days, as lies and death made war, against life and truth. Whatever else happened, no one was going to try to hurt her Momma anymore, not without getting past She-wolf, first!

They reached a wider little plateau upon the ridge peak, about half-way up the long ridge to their cave. It was just about sunset, and Adam, knowing that everyone was tired and hungry, called a halt, and they went to the far end of the little ledge, which was roughly 20 feet by 60 feet, and there they sat down, leaning their backs against a few little boulders there, while they munched some snacks, and watched the beautiful sunset, which was stunning, with high western fiery red clouds, and brilliant oranges, and purples, which chased after the sun, as a fading east wind blew the evening storm out to the west, with the sun. The wolves ate some of their things, and curled up next to the people to nap.

As the sun faded, all of their eyelids grew heavy, and they all four fell asleep, as darkness deepened. The humans had on buckskins, and they also had on thick fur coats, as did the wolves. The rocks shielded them from the cool breeze, and the fur and the body heat from the giant pile of all of them made them feel toasty and snug.

As they rested, Adam suddenly saw King Jesus in his dreams, and King Jesus said to him, "Adam, in a minute, I will wake you up, and Eve, too, and I will show you a far-away-in-time descendent of yours, one of your many-times-great-grandsons. This man is one of My favorites. He listens to My visions, and he will tell the truth about Me to everyone that he can. Do not reveal that you see him, since he really will be physically present with you, but I wish him to wonder if it is a vision, a dream, or a real space-time event. That lingering mystery in his heart will keep him forever curious, and keep him seeking more marvels, which I will share with him, later."

"When you awake, after you build your evening fire, be very sure to leave your two flints right beside the fire rocks, easy to spot. They will one day become a unique inheritance for this grandson of yours!"

Instantly, just as King Jesus finished speaking, Adam woke fully, and sat up, and Eve also instantly woke, and sat up with him, looking into the darkness, which was not total, since a full moon had risen a bit above the horizon. The two wolves instantly woke also, in perfect sync with their people, and all of them stared down toward the far end of the little ledge.

A strange man was there in the dark, looking in their direction, and he seemed to suddenly spot them. Instinctively, Adam and Eve each found their hands already holding their huge knives, each knife carved from the tooth of a T-rex. As the humans slowly started to rise, the stranger dropped flat to the ground, and then rolled to his side, squirming behind some small boulders there, near to one edge.

Wolf snarled, and his upper lip curled back, and his hackles rose up like a lion's mane around his neck, and his ears went back flat, as a deep war growl rumbled in his chest. As he sprang up to his feet, he heard Adam say, "Easy, Wolf, he is one of us! Don't scare him. Pretend you are looking for something else!"

Wolf trotted over near the hiding man, and deliberately looked away from him, making himself not growl, and forcibly commanding his hackles to settle down again. Wolf picked up a couple of large sticks, instead, and trotted back jauntily to Adam with them. As he drew near, Adam laughed, and said, "Okay, Wolf, so you proved me wrong again! Maybe we can find enough small brush up here, from old dead trees and such, and maybe we can cook and stay warm tonight, too. Good boy!"

As they all stood up, and started to move toward the place where Wolf found the firewood, Adam told Eve, "This man is our distant grandson. We do not want to scare him, so pretend that we do not see him."

They gathered enough wood, and Adam built a little log-cabin-style fire, and then he gently took a little under fur from Wolf and She-wolf, without hurting them, and made a little spark nest in the center of the kindling. Then, he took out his favorite two fire-flints, and the iron striking rock that he also carried. He held the twin flints in one hand, near the spark nest, and struck them with the iron rod, until a shower of sparks flew into the spark nest, and began to kindle the fur. Then he softly whispered into the little fire, commanding it to grow larger, and it did. Soon, they were all delighting in its' merry blaze, and the glorious warmth in the chilly night air. They got out their additional food stuffs, and cooked some of the things like potatoes on sticks over the fire, until they were nice and ready, while the wolves filled up again on the carnivore tree fruit, and chewed happily upon some of its' delicious (at least to them) branches.

After they were all well filled, and content, they snuggled up together again for the long night ahead. It was only about 9:00 o'clock, but they were tired. In the early morning, they would have to get moving, since it was still a full day's climb, the rest of the way up to their winter cave.

Meanwhile, the stranger listened silently from the other side of the little boulders where they all were. Eve felt sorry for him, and worried that he might be cold. She almost got up to put a fur over him, to help keep him warm, but Adam felt her start to move, and reached out a hand, and he gently grabbed her wrist, as she was reaching for one of their extra furs, and, looking at her calmly, but very seriously, deep in her eyes, he shook his head slightly "no". Eve had learned, through very painful events in the

Garden, and the results thereof, that it was usually best not to argue with Adam. She smiled slightly, nodded, sighed, and relaxed with her head on his chest, as she snuggled close to him for warmth, and they all drifted off.

At about 4:00 A.M., Adam was suddenly awakened by the Lord, and he smoothly stood up, letting Eve sleep a few more minutes, while he quietly packed up everything they carried, and then he went over close to the fire, wondering if he should extinguish it, since there was no forest up in these rocks to catch fire, after all. Maybe their grandson would wake up after they left, and find the coals warm, at least.

Adam noticed his two flints lying there in the dirt, easily visible in the moonlight, since they were white flint. He started to reach out his hand, to pick them up, and then he stopped, remembering the Lord's request. Adam looked up into Heaven, and smiled, and said, "Very well, Lord!

Tonight, we will leave the boy an inheritance from his most ancient relative!"

As he stood back up straight, Adam heard King Jesus say in his mind, "Quite true, even if he will have to wait for 780,000 years to receive it!"

Adam noticed that Eve was not only up and also packed to go, but the wolves were up and quietly stretching, ready to get moving as well. Before Adam could object, just as they were starting to follow the wolves toward the far end of the ledge, to continue their upward climb, Eve smoothly and swiftly stepped over to their sleeping grandson, and leaned quickly down, and lightly brushed his unconscious cheek with a grandmotherly kiss. The man did not stir, and Eve danced past Adam, and trotted after the two wolves, which were already moving out along the ridge pathway.

Eve knew that Adam had said not to scare or disturb the man, and she had not.

Nevertheless, no one, not even her beloved husband, was going to keep Eve from kissing her grandson! (It was too late for Adam to stop her, anyway.)

PRESSURE-COOKED

How does it feel, to be buried under millions of tons of granite? What about if the ambient temperature is so hot (hundreds, or thousands, of degrees) that instant explosive ignition would occur, if any oxygen were available, to allow burning? How does it feel to be kept there, for millions of years?

Even though that might sound, to some folks, like any ordinary day in the life of a sincere Christian, such unimaginable conditions are the difference between a lump of coal, and a diamond. If a lump of coal is set on a sidewalk, and crushed, it produces only coal dust. The lump in question must be contained within a structure surrounding it, which maintains its' static shape, as the off-scale pressures and super-high temperatures remain active, for a very long time. Those things produce jewels, not dust.

The structure surrounding the particular lump will also usually be more of the same coal, also subjected to similar pressures and temperatures. Not every lump is allowed to endure, and be transformed into a diamond. Otherwise, we would find vast deposits of huge, single-piece, solid diamonds, weighing hundreds of tons apiece. Instead, we find a few diamonds scattered and concealed in a lot of coal dust.

None of the jewelers in the world display lumps of coal, or coal dust, in the glass cases. Only those rare victorious lumps (now called "diamonds", once they have graduated, from Coal Dust University) are valued enough to have bright lights shine upon them, and to have experts examine them closely through magnified lenses, searching for imperfections. Nobody spends several months' worth of money for coal dust. No woman wants to wear a raw lump of coal on her finger, or hang a crude lump from each ear lobe.

A good way to phrase this concept might be, "No victory, no value." That might sound a bit harsh, unless the whole point of the operation is to produce victorious, bright jewels.

There is a warning in Peter to not think it strange, concerning the fiery trial which awaits us. This is what purifies our faith, as fine gold is purified in a crucible, with fire. This refined faith is the treasure which is dearest unto our Heavenly Father, among all of the attributes which are required by Him in the nature of each of His children. (Remember, after we have suffered a while, our God will, Himself, restore us!) This refined faith can only be founded upon a genuine love of God, or else, the follower would give up too soon. Demonstrating one's love for God not only includes how we bless our brothers and sisters, present and future, but it also includes how we persevere in our race to follow King Jesus all the Way home, to Heaven. At times, it is a sprint, but it always resumes as an endless marathon, in between sprints! We are told that the Finish Line is all well worth it.

As an extension of the analogy, once the process, however necessarily painful, for the one being processed, has been completed, the finished product is a thing of wonder and beauty, and possesses new abilities and qualities which would never have been at all possible, unless the ordeal had been endured, and conquered.

Diamonds are bright and sparkly, dazzling in brilliance, and universally admired. As the so-called "hardest substance known to man" diamonds can be used in astonishing applications. They are extremely useful in technology, science, medicine, and heavy industry. They never seem to return to coal dust, either. The phenomenal changes in the diamond are one-way, permanent enhancements, which could only be crafted by the wisdom and power of Almighty God, and, once created, cannot ever be destroyed, except by Almighty God.

Now of course, with modern science and technology, mankind can imitate the good Lord, and make artificial diamonds, at will, and to precise specs, but it was still God that invented them. God invented lightning long before mankind invented wall outlets, too.

(These days we can also destroy diamonds, too. Just strap them to a nuclear bomb. The result is not diamond dust, or even diamond vapor. It is plasma, and immediately it forgets that it ever was a diamond, or anything but plasma.)

Diamonds do not only reflect light, but they also pass light through them. Often, in the case with high-quality jewels, little loss of light occurs, even if it is often scattered into many colors, through the prism. What started as dull, dark dust became marvelous, stunning crystal, permanent in glory, and a delight to the eye and soul.

Since the Lord is the Father of Lights, we should perhaps try to reflect more light unto others. Maybe we should also practice trying to allow His true Light of brotherly, humble love to shine through us into the hearts of others. We should probably not give up, until we have finished being pressure-cooked, all the Way, until we are fully done. This week is Thanksgiving, and no one wants their turkeys suddenly deciding for themselves that they have cooked long enough, and then trying to jump out of the oven! God will know when it is precisely the right time, even if we cannot tell until it happens.

It will likely encourage the faith and hope in our other brothers and sisters, when they see some of us endure patiently, with unyielding faith and trust. Try to remember, the required conditions may often include something like tons of pressure, for a long, hot, miserable time. Try to out wait it, and beat the temptation to quit. Three things are certain about the future: (1) God will still be God, (2) God will still be good, and (3) God will still be alive, and well!

If you want to get bonus style-points for it, try not to squirm around too much. The diamond forms quicker, larger, more perfectly, and with fewer flaws, if the entire setting remains undisturbed by anything disruptive, such as an Earthquake. The trembling ground is not your responsibility, but your being patient to overcome is. "In your patience possess your souls."

People rate four qualities of diamonds: (1) carat, (2) clarity, (3) color, and (4) cut. Of all of those, mankind has a vote in pretty much only the cut. Even after the diamond has endured all of the heat and pressure, and the rough polishing, it still has to be cut, and then fine polished.

Even after all of that, diamonds are to be marked with little numbers etched into them by lasers, for identity purposes. They are also documented by an expert, using a magnified lens, and he makes a chart of the unique flaws, cracks, or any other type of small imperfections in the jewel. Now, technology has simplified it so that machines usually can do the examination and charting even faster and more accurately than humans, which also is the best way to laser-etch it.

So, it seems that the final product still has a lot of finish work, even after becoming a diamond. When finally done, the stone is unique, and registered, and recorded, and traceable. We should continue to try to be patient and bear good fruit, while the final touches are being done. We are being transformed into beautiful, unique, one-of-a-kind precious jewels, and being made into something of great worth, instead of the trash which we once were.

Also, try to be encouraged by the fact that there is a fifth way that mankind identifies the finished diamonds. Even the flaws are useful, and they inhabit each stone in an individual, personalized pattern, as unique as snowflakes.

Also, try to remember that the stone is no less a diamond, and no less valuable, just because it has a flaw or two. Even King Jesus wore the scars and marks from His Own wounds, and those particular marks were absolutely unique unto Him. The disciples saw and recorded the remaining scars and wounds. He even left us the Shroud of Turin, and the marks upon it, as additional proof of His wounds, and their unique pattern, which is One-of-a King!

THE VIEW FROM INSIDE THE UNIFIED FIELD

Some fellows named Euclid, Pythagoras, Archimedes, Galileo, Copernicus, Newton, Kepler, Maxwell, Marconi, Einstein, Bohr, Fermi, and Oppenheimer, along with many, many others, less famous (or more top-secret), have opened up our understandings of precisely how all the physical aspects of Creation are assembled.

Just when they thought they all had it all about figured out, along came Mandelbrot, a most unusual human being, even among elite geniuses. He has been gifted with a mind which actually can directly perceive the mathematical formulae of advanced geometric shapes and figures. When he looks at a mathematic formula, the shape of the thing it describes pops into his inner view screen, in his mind, in crystal-clear 3D.

He can rotate it to any angle of view, zoom in and out, and even look out from the inside of the shape, whether it is a sphere, a cone, a cube, a tetrahedron, or a dodecahedron. These sorts of unusual abilities enabled him to perceive the hidden-right-in-front-of-our-noses, universally ubiquitous, all-saturating phenomenon of fractal mathematics.

What directs the pattern of waves breaking upon the shore, the structure of clouds, the number of bifurcations of the branches of a tree, and their spacing along the trunk of the tree, as well as the ratio of tall trees to short trees in a forest is all determined by fractal math patterns. This principle extends all the way to the mega-structures of Creation, including the shapes of spiral galaxies, and the clustering of large groups of galaxies in systems so enormous that human minds struggle to grasp the scale.

One of the most fascinating aspects of fractal geometric shapes is how a very rugged coastline cannot be accurately measured for precise length, but, using fractal math, a very close final value can be determined, of the coastline's "roughness". The greater the roughness, the greater will be the length.

Another feature is that if a shape's outer surface is broken into angles, and this is carried to a far enough extreme, the distance around the outer surface approaches infinity, even though the entire total area within the shape remains about the same.

Brain scientists have remained puzzled to this day as to how an organ no larger than a three-pound human brain can store such vast amounts of information, and process such enormous volumes of data, at such rapid rates. Until the recent development of ultra-fast supercomputers, the human brain had remained king of all known processors.

That's not all. How can a subsystem of that brain, a section called the hippocampus, store a lifetime's worth of extremely detailed, intense memories, in a region the size of a walnut?

How can a brain learn new things, and remember, and recall them? The finest supercomputers, with the most advanced artificial intelligence programs, still have a lot of trouble trying to learn. Even a newborn baby human does that, and well.

Of course, one of the simple explanations is that human minds were designed and built by Almighty God. He did such a fine job that we can even use our minds to build artificial minds, but we still cannot even come close to the outrageous magnificence of the human brain. It is pretty obvious that we never will.

It is interesting how our good Lord places clues right there in front of us, and yet we go along for centuries, without noticing them. The Word of God declares that God has set eternity in the hearts of men. If anyone else has ever experienced the time-dilation effect, that's where you find yourself suddenly in the middle of a motorcycle wreck, but all of it is moving in very slow motion, or somebody in a bar takes a swing at your face, but it seems to move through molasses, and there is lots of time to dodge, or block, and all day long to return fire.

Our modern understanding of time indicates that the flow of time is always, and always will be, forward, but at various rates, depending upon the condition, vector, velocity, and perception of the observer, in relation to the surrounding environment. Time slows to a crawl when one approaches the speed of light. This might lead us to the projected conclusion that time stops for anything moving at the speed of light, but it does not, or light photons would freeze in place.

But, back to the space to storage ratio puzzle, about our gray matter, the apparent answer is that the architecture of the brain is entirely based upon fractal math structures, which may seem less logical than straight cubical matrix type structure, but allows for vastly increased efficiency in storage capacity. The fractal branches, incorporating the inherent fractal aspects of infinite repetition, plus self-similarity, produce nearly infinite volume within the limited physical space, by effectively folding space back upon itself, many times over, and all without the use of a gravitational singularity! Only Almighty God could have invented a design principle like that, and put a spark of awareness in it, and made it able to think, and to learn, and to remember, too.

Therefore, the strange structure of the neurons and synapses is able to function in some manners as though it were no longer constrained by ordinary space and time. The brain can do a huge spectrum of things which it should not ever be able to do. Even if it could, the thing should be about forty stories tall.

Einstein was obsessed with a futile search for a unified field, something which saturated all of time and space, and, once discovered, would unite in all aspects both relativity and quantum physics. The math for this "field" did not seem to fit both scenarios, large structures and subatomic, since one set of rules worked in one case, but not another.

Gravity ruled the large structures, following fractal math patterns. At the subatomic level, gravity was the least strong of all the four detectable forces. Strong nuclear, weak nuclear, and electromagnetic were much bigger players in the subatomic realm.

Remember that God often hides the answers right in front of our noses, waiting for us to notice them. Even though fractal math pervades and thoroughly saturates all of nature, no one even noticed it until Mandelbrot. Gravity also pervades and saturates all of Creation, but it is so ubiquitous, no one even noticed it, until Isaac Newton did.

What seems to be the logical next step is that the "universal field" has already been discovered, and it is gravity! There is no place in the universe where gravity is not present. Gravity is always attractive, never repulsive. Gravity, in marked opposite to the other forces, has no upper limit, and requires no source generator.

Electromagnetism can be intensified, to unimaginable densities, but always requires a generating source. Even the electromagnetic blast from an EMP bomb has to be formed by a nuclear-powered generator, in the form of a detonation.

Gravity does not have to be generated, it just exists. Nothing is exempted from its' authority. Anything with any physical mass is under its' crown. Even light, which supposedly cannot be slowed down, and weighs nothing, is held captive by strong enough concentrations of gravity.

The reason why scientists cannot unite what happens inside a black hole with either normal space time relativity, or with quantum mechanics, is that when gravity becomes concentrated to the point where it holds light captive, all other forces cease to matter at all. A large fraction of this effect occurs even in neutron stars, where strong, weak, and electro forces cease to be able to keep the matter in the normal structure of atoms and molecules, and it all degrades into neutrons. Scientists need to stop searching for what is right in front of them, and see that gravity is actually the legendary unified field that they are hunting all over to find.

In similar manner, brain scientists should realize that the pathways of our minds are designed upon fractal principles, and then perhaps they will be able to plot or chart, or at least accurately observe the detailed patterns of human thought. There is one part that will escape their grasp, however.

The part of the human awareness that can believe in God, and experience faith, and knowledge of the Most High, will never be contained in a test tube. That is the part of us that is most self-similar unto our Heavenly Father, since He made us in His image. That's why eternity is set in the hearts of men, and why the rate of time flow is always subjective for the individual person, no matter what your watch says!

MERCY WITH TEETH

(This story is based upon actual real events which happened in Yellowstone, as documented in the PBS special "In the Valley of the Wolves".)

In the Lamar Valley, the hunting was always the best. It was the choice region for any wolf pack to occupy, since the rivers and vegetation automatically guided many animals there, of the various types that numbered among the favorite items on the wolf menu. Deer, elk, and many others were usually not too much effort to find and harvest. Water was available, and shelter was abundant in the surrounding hills. When it came time for pups, open fields would not do. A den in a cave was the preference.

The Lamar pack was strong, with many tough young wolves, and a fierce and seasoned Alpha leader, which routinely drove off other wolves trying to invade his precious home turf. There was a young black-furred male that was not actually part of that pack, but was a love-struck lone wolf. This male was called "305". He was courting the daughter of the Alpha pair, the wolf-princess of the clan, so to speak. She liked him back, but Papa was not going to have any of it, and the older wolf drove off the young hopeful, and told him in plain wolf-talk to stay away from his daughter!

Not too long after that, the older Alpha wolf passed away, and a couple of months after that, so did his widow. The Lamar pack was led now by a much more inexperienced wolf, one of the sons of the Alpha pair, but he was not yet seasoned enough in battle tactics and kill-or-be-killed experience to hold the Lamar Valley against strong invaders, which were a rugged pack from Slough Creek, located just a few miles away.

The Slough pack drove the Lamar pack out of their home valley, and made them exiles into the regions around the Valley. The Sloughs kept harassing the Lamars, whenever they tried to return into the valley, and this usurping abomination continued for over a year.

During that time, the Lamars were still having pups, growing stronger, and quietly becoming a mighty clan once again, out of sight of the Sloughs. The strength of a pack is not only the strong mighty adult fighters and hunters, but also the pups, without which the pack will not long survive, since the older wolves die off in time.

Of course, the Sloughs were still having many pups, too. They had been stronger to start with, when they had managed to conquer the Lamars, and they had just as many new pups coming along as did the Lamars.

The Sloughs were overfilled with their pride, and thought that they could do anything they wanted, to any body they wanted, and they stupidly believed that even Almighty God could not stop them. They proved that they thought this one day, when a single male coyote, trying to scavenge a scrap of food for himself and his sweet little mate, made the unfortunate mistake of sneaking up to grab a little piece of the leftovers from the recent wolf-kill, since he had waited patiently, until all of the wolves had eaten their fill, and were lazing around digesting their meals.

They watched like they did not care, until he actually took a tiny scrap, and then six of the crazier, meaner ones launched themselves like rockets after him. They scared him, all right, and the poor little guy dropped the scrap, and ran for his life, but the huge wolves, even with full stomachs, had much longer, stronger legs, and they ran him down. They could have just run him off. That was all that the Lamars had ever done to him, before. But these were the evil Sloughs. All six of the wolves jumped on the helpless little thirty pound coyote, and each of them weighed over a hundred pounds, and they ripped him to shreds, without killing him cleanly first. The murdering bastards did not realize that the documentary film crew was watching, and caught the whole atrocity on film.

Others were watching, also. The shocked and broken-hearted little mate of the helpless coyote watched him being murdered. She was carrying three of his babies inside her, next to her broken heart.

Still others were watching, too. King Jesus and Wolf were standing side by side, looking down from the viewing porch of the Palace. A nearly sub-sonic deep rumble was coming from Wolf's throat, just loud enough to hear, but it made goose bumps form to those who heard it, and put a deep shiver into their souls. There was something about Wolf which most people did not realize. He was like Adam. Wolf had never been born, since he was an original, prototype creature, one of the first-made, from the actual Garden of Eden.

Wolves are the kings of canines, and that includes all canines, all over the Earth. Among all wolves, only the first-created wolf, the original, would ever be allowed to be king. When it came to Alpha males, Wolf was indeed both Alpha and Omega, since he had been resurrected into an eternal wolf, and was the perfect original, and there would never be any new and improved models after him. This particular Wolf was the King of Wolves, and the King of Canines, too.

When King Jesus heard the deep rumble in Wolf's throat, He looked over at him, and said, "I know, Wolf. I see them, too. Go and pick out your most deadly wolves, your toughest, and strongest, and smartest, and select them out until you have one dozen wolves, the best of the best, and report back here to me with them in six months. It will be deep winter in Yellowstone then, and I will have this matter set right at that time. I will provide for and defend the coyote's mate and his soon-to-be-born pups. For right now, please go welcome our little friend the coyote, since I want him here now, with us, to watch while we avenge him!"

"First, let him know you mean him no harm, and then, take him to the chow hall, and show him that not all wolves are evil!" King Jesus watched while Wolf trotted obediently away to follow orders, tail wagging once again, since he had been given the promise that vengeance would soon be executed upon the evil Sloughs.

The King of Wolves took it very personally whenever some of his own kind did horrible things. Killing to eat, instead of starving, well, that was one thing, but killing someone that was helpless, just because the murderers were evil in their hearts, was an inexcusable crime. Not only would they have to pay, but their descendents would pay it back, also, since the adults stole the father of the coyote puppies, even before they were born. An eye for an eye, a tooth for a tooth, and a family for a family, was the Law of Justice.

What they had done unto others would soon be done unto them. Wolf would begin his screening selection tomorrow. First, he had a new friend to welcome.

Time passed both upon Earth, and in Heaven. The coyote puppies were born, a far way off from the cursed evil Sloughs, and lived long and happy lives in a new zone, with their mother, and some other coyotes that they met. The Lamars continued to survive and grow, but still remained essentially nomadic, always longing to return home to their precious valley. The Sloughs seemed like they

TOO GOOD TO BE UNTRUE

were still growing stronger, too, and there seemed little hope that the Lamars could ever conquer them.

Six months after he had received the special assignment from King Jesus, Wolf arrived upon the observation porch of the Palace, bringing a dozen enormous wolves with him, all of them nearly as large and strong as he was. They all bowed before King Jesus, and then He told them to sit up, and to listen very closely. He went on to tell them that no insane little band of animals was going to deliberately work perverse evil against helpless victims, and then escape justice. Such things were a disgrace not only to all the noble and good wolves that ever lived, but it was also an abomination and an offense unto King Jesus, personally, when anyone used their greater strength to oppress and harm a weaker person. Yes, it did matter unto Almighty King Jesus that a little coyote was murdered unfairly. King Jesus then spent a few more seconds telling them specifically what He wanted them to do, and do no more beyond that. The rest could wait until the fire.

Then King Jesus called the little coyote over to them, and introduced them all, and said, "Now, I name you Scandalon, the Greek word for bait. I will cause your lost life to become poison bait unto the evil Sloughs, which murdered you. Watch, while Wolf and his assault team avenge your life!"

King Jesus looked at Wolf, smiled, and shouted, "Go!"

Instantly, Wolf and the dozen killers with him stretched their mighty wings, and launched like streaking missiles toward the Earth. As soon as they launched, their fur, on each of them, except for Wolf himself, turned instantly jet black. God would not send white wolves to kill, since they were sent as the messengers of death. Wolf remained white, because it was his permanent glory, as King of Wolves.

Within a few minutes, they all landed together, at the foot of the steep hill containing the cave which the Sloughs had chosen for their den. The cave was about two-thirds of the way up the hillside, about 100 feet up, and a steep, rocky path led up to the entrance. There was no sign of the Sloughs, which were all out hunting, even the hungry mother wolves, and they felt so over-confident that they thought that nothing would dare to menace their pups.

Wolf spoke to his team, just before they took the action which they were sent here to do. He reminded them, "We have been sent to perform our King's will, precisely as He has commanded us. We will obey Him. Steel your hearts now, and set your resolve. No matter how much it hurts you inside, to hear the cries of the dying pups, you must not be deterred. You are to take up a blockade position across the entrance to the cave, and you will instantly kill any of the adult Sloughs which try to enter. You will not enter their cave yourselves, at all, and you will not hurt any of the pups which try to crawl out. Nevertheless, you are required to use your noses to nudge the puppies back inside the cave, until it is over. Let none escape, and let none enter."

As he finished his orders, all twelve of the assault team wolves turned as one, and began the climb up the steep path to the cave. A few minutes later, they arrived, and took up positions all along the little ledge that ran across the entrance to the cave, and this formed a single line of wolves, all black (which made them pop out in sharp contrast to the white snow all over the hillside), stretching about 80 feet along the full length of the ledge. There was no way around them, and it would be unwise to try to break through. The twelve remained openly visible, although with their enormous wings folded out of sight. They each found his own particular spot, evenly spaced apart, and then they settled in, to do what a mortal wolf might try to do, but likely could not.

They all knew that they were going to sit motionless, right where they had settled, for 14 solid days and nights, without moving to even eat, or perform normal bodily functions. Eternal wolves were unbreakable, just like the good angels.

Soon after the team settled in, the Sloughs arrived, trotting ignorantly home, carrying huge chunks of meat to shred for the puppies. As they came around the bend and saw the hillside, they stopped, shocked, and even dropped the chunks of meat from their open maws, a thing which is very rare for a wild wolf.

The thing that they saw made their hearts fail, and their skin crawl, even under their thick fur, and a deep fear and chill seized their minds, when they saw the huge strangers up by their cave. They instantly thought that their pups were already dead. A couple of the younger mother wolves started to rush toward the foot of the path, but were tackled by three of the big males, and snarled at to hold still. The females whined in fear and frustration, until the big Alpha snarled fiercely at them, making them stop.

He was not going to lead his pack into a strange situation, against unknown enemies, without at least a few moments scouting and planning. His eyes scanned the assault team, and he saw all twelve, but not Wolf, which had hidden himself from their eyes, although he was standing right in front of them. The Alpha Slough knew at a glance that something was extremely different about those wolves. Most other wolves just seemed like an easy challenge for him, but he was somehow terrified of even one of those monsters. Nonetheless, he remembered that his entire pack was watching him closely, to see if he had turned coward. He began to take a step or two toward the pathway.

Suddenly, he froze, and dropped to the ground, tail tucked, hiding his face under his paws, and he curled up like a little puppy, and he began whining softly, and trembling violently, in sudden mortal fear.

Where this usually would be a great disgrace before all of his pack, this time it did not matter, since every one of them had just done precisely the same things. They moaned and howled softly, in terror.

The trigger for all of this reaction was that suddenly, they had all heard a very deep, nearly sub-sonic growl that sounded like a mean volcano about to explode. The intensity of that growl was so strong, that it actually shook the ground under their feet a little bit.

That would have done it, but the thing which really made them all cringe in fear was that the air around them was suddenly filled with the overwhelming scent of the King of Wolves. The growl of their King had brought them all down to the ground, but the thick reality of his scent was like a knife straight into the mind of each wolf, that this was very real, and they all were about to die!

After a few minutes, Wolf quietly and invisibly flew up to the ledge, to join his team, but it was hours before any of the Sloughs moved at all, since they still smelled traces of his scent around them. It made their bone marrow turn to ice.

For the next two solid weeks, day and night, the Sloughs watched helplessly, while the team held its' ground. The wolves in the team had to endure hearing the sad cries of the dying pups, but they were soldiers, and knew it was part of the good Lord's plan. They hated this part, but knew that He would set it all right soon. King Jesus was not only working out His perfect justice, but He was also showing mercy, to the Sloughs, adults and dying pups, alike, and also, to the Lamars. As each of the puppies died of thirst, or cold, the little soul was rushed up to Heaven, where the new arrival was placed into the care of one of the mates of the members of the assault team. When these soldier wolves finished their grim task, and returned home, each one of them would find a brand new adopted son or daughter to love in Heaven! These baby pups would never be cold or starving or thirsty to death, for all eternity, after this.

At the end of the two weeks, when the last of the Slough pups had been gone for three full days, the black killer team walked calmly and quietly down the path, keeping their wings hidden, and then disappeared into the forest, never to be seen again, by the Sloughs. The Sloughs watched them go, with a fearful shiver, and then, without any thought at all of vengeance, sadly walked up the path, to confirm what they already knew, that all of their puppies were dead.

A few months after, in late February, many wolves were going around seeking mates from other clans, to try to start their own clans. This was also the season when entire packs made their territorial moves, and both love and war filled the landscape in Yellowstone. The Sloughs had lost their Alpha male, when he was killed by mountain lions, and also the second-in-command, his brother, was killed by them, a few days later.

One fine early March morning, with a lot of snow still carpeting the ground, the entire Lamar pack decided that it was time to move back home. While the Sloughs had been wasting away ever since the deaths of their pups (which had broken their spirits) the Lamars had been growing rapidly, and now had many strong young wolves to bring into battle, and a group of yearlings and puppies, also. The Lamars outnumbered the Sloughs, now, and more of the Lamars were combat-ready war wolves, spoiling for a fight.

The Lamars were led back down into the Valley, back into the zone of their enemies, to reclaim their own stolen home. The new Alpha male which they followed had earned their respect and love in the hardest ways imaginable, keeping the pack alive, and thriving, and growing stronger, even while still in exile, for over two years. The Lamars loved their leader, and would give life for him any day.

As the solid black Alpha male led his pack home, beside him trotted his mate, the one he had always loved, who had been the princess of the old royal pair. They already had four pups, which tried to keep up with their long-legged mother. The same black wolf, "305", had grown up mighty, and mature, and responsible, for the lives of almost thirty wolves, which trusted and followed him without question.

As the females turned aside at the edge of the Valley, to wait out the battle while guarding the young, all of the 14 combat-ready males followed 305 at full speed, as they slammed with killing fury into the Sloughs. A wonderful coincidence was that the new Lamar Alpha was just as jet-black as the killer team wolves had been, and in his rage, he seemed about as huge and ferocious! The Sloughs thought for a moment that one of those unbreakable monsters was the one leading the fierce attack!

Without their two toughest fighters, the now-dead Alpha, and his also-dead brother, the Sloughs did not have any champions that could stand against the 305. He carved into them like a chainsaw, ripping open wounds they would remember for the rest of their defeated lives. It was all over, in less than six minutes. All of the Sloughs were wounded, and four were dead. Those four concluded the list of the wolves which had murdered the little coyote. The survivors fled at full speed for their lives, never to challenge the Lamars in their Valley again. As they fled, the Lamars chased them all the way completely out of the Valley, for over twenty miles, nipping at their heels all the way. (In time, the losses suffered by the Sloughs would teach them humility, and their hearts would turn, and never again would they kill for sport, or anger. Once repented, they could be forgiven.)

A few hours later, the victors returned back, and the whole pack gathered, at the site of their old main den. They waited excitedly, but respectfully, until 305 threw his mighty head back, and sent forth a triumphant howl that shook the icy air, and carried all the way to the ears of the still running Sloughs. All of the Lamars joined joyfully in, at once, even the little pups! This was the celebration to end all celebrations, as even the wolves praised our good Lord for His infinite fair justice, and His everlasting mercy!

Upon the observation deck of the Palace, King Jesus looked over to Wolf, and said, "Now, do you see? I would not leave such an offense unanswered."

Then, He looked over to Scandalon, the little coyote, and asked, "Are you content, for now?"

Scandalon wagged his tail, and yipped, "Yes!"

THE BOTTOMLESS PIT

The archeologist was back in the U.S. for a short vacation home, to visit with some family members. For the last few years, he had spent all of his time in Israel, finding amazing ancient relics, and causing quite a stir among all the other archeologists in the Middle East. He seemed to keep finding things that confirmed the precision of the accounts recorded in the Holy Scriptures. His Hebrew and Christian associates thought of him as a modern hero, but the Muslim side despised him, and had even begun to consider placing a price upon his life. Wherever he went in Israel, he always had his wolf, his gray donkey, and also, a pistol, a rifle, and two machine guns. Even more importantly, he carried and read his Bible, every day.

He had first spent a few days with the majority of his family, catching up and celebrating, and then he had gone down to Houston, to visit his brother, a NASA scientist, and a key design team leader in the new "Space Launch System". (This was the single huge rocket which NASA had chosen over the abandoned Constellation program, which had planned to utilize two rockets of essentially identical-twin design, except that one was much larger than the other. That concept had been to use the small rocket to launch only the crews, but the larger rocket to launch major equipment for use in lunar exploration.)

Since NASA had already begun testing the J-2X second stage rocket engine, successfully, and also the Multi-Purpose Orion Crew Capsule, he wanted to see some of the new things in progress, while combining the time visiting his very busy brother. They had always been close, and saw each other too seldom, since he had moved over to work in Israel. He took a cab from the airport to the front gate at

NASA, and got out, to find that his brother had sent a car over to pick him up, and bring him out to the lab. As he rode the final leg of the journey, he reflected about how different life was, between here, in the thick of the U.S. military industrial complex, and out in the wild areas of Israel, alone with his wolf, his donkey, and of course, his wonderful Lord, King Jesus.

As he was led into the lab complex, he walked through many security barriers, escorted by an armed guard all the way, until he was finally in the outer office of his brother, where the nice receptionist led him on in to meet with his sibling, who was still talking with intensity and animation with someone on the phone. He motioned for him to have a seat, and then concluded with, "Well, I still think we can have it working in the next year, and we ought to hold the final design for the new processor until then, once I can finish the configuration and tests on it.

My brother's here now, so I'll call you back Monday about it. Okay, later."

As he hung up, he jumped up, ran around his desk, grabbed his big brother in a bear hug, and said, "Man, it's good to see you! You're getting stronger, and more tan by about two zones, the way Ansel Adams would rate it."

The Archeologist laughed, and replied, "Well, that happens when you spend your days and nights out doors, climbing rocks and hunting for things out in the middle of nowhere."

His brother answered, "Yeah, congratulations on being the most controversial archeologist since Indiana Jones! I bet you don't go visiting any mosques when you're over there."

The man replied, "No, usually I'm out in the field, or at the University, examining a relic, but when I stay in town, I mostly keep to myself, and rest, and also study more of the Dead Sea Scrolls, now that they are being released more and more. I do still try to keep up with the sciences, though, since the more we discover, the more it proves the truth of God's Word."

The scientist replied, "Amen, Brother! Now, let's go eat lunch. We have an excellent lunchroom here, and we serve more than just astronaut food."

The men went and ate, and continued to catch up on the latest and greatest news that each one had to share, and this covered a span of more than two years, since they had last spoken, face to face. They chatted about all the other family members, and then described the more complicated details of what each other's professional activities currently produced.

The archeologist told him about the details of finding Adam's own two fire-flints, and the vision-experience of seeing the first family there upon the ledge. His brother listened, captivated and stunned, and asked many excited, eager questions about it all, as they walked back to the office.

Next, he told him about finding the fragile surviving fragment of the jawbone of an ass, the same jawbone that Samson had used to kill over a thousand Philistine warriors in a single day. Then he described the vision-experience that was manifested, where he actually watched for hours as Samson killed hundreds and hundreds of brutal Philistines, and their dead and dying bodies piled up down below him at the base of the sloping ridge where he stood his ground, and held it, against the enemies of the people of God.

His brother, although a scientist, was just as much a sincere Christian as the archeologist, but had always loved the technical aspects of modern civilization, and especially loved inventing new materials, and ways of using them. After he had had a time to absorb the wonder of the special supernatural experiences which had been granted unto his brother, he ventured a hesitant comment. He said, slowly, "Well, I know that you always had the most vivid and intense dreams of anyone in our family, but, sometimes, I am convinced that our good Lord sends things unto me that way, too, and sometimes the answer to a problem just sort of forms in my mind, and I suddenly see it! Now, I am not dumb, but that can only be the Lord!"

His big brother laughed a hearty laugh, and said, "Now, you know what it feels like, too! Do some of your colleagues tilt their heads, and ask, very concerned, if you're feeling all right?"

The brothers shared a laugh over that common response which is frequently the reward given unto the visionary. They both agreed that it was still well worth the hassle, since the dreams and visions always proved out to be accurate, and precisely correct, if they were ones sent by the good Lord. The counterfeit ones sent by the enemy never came true, and, over the years, each man had learned ways to discern if the message was authentically from King Jesus, or not. For one thing, no lying spirit from hell could ever admit that King Jesus Christ was truly the Only Begotten, Holy Son of God, and that God had raised Him from the dead. Only a messenger from Heaven could acknowledge that fact as truth.

The scientist then related his own research into graphene, a new material developed from an ancient material. Lead is a layered mineral, and can be split in half along the layers, again and again and again, until a layer only a single molecule thick is left, which is formed into a large, flat sheet of graphene. This material conducts electricity with zero loss, at near-light speed, with no heat by-product. (Essentially, it acts like a super-conductor, but at room temperature, instead of near absolute zero.) The research teams were already designing and making the first elements to be used in the new ultra-processors for the new space craft designs, which would be far more dependable, rugged, low-cost, durable in all temperatures, and also, most importantly, could be fabricated into tiny ultra-computers which could pilot a spacecraft all the way from Earth orbit to a safe, soft landing upon the moon. The new materials would allow a computer smaller than a dime to do what an IBM system named Deep Blue had once done, to beat the human World Champion, at chess.

"If we have time tomorrow, I want to take you over to meet my friend, Franklin Chang-Diaz, who is the inventor and developer of the new VASIMR rocket engines, which can generate as much as 100-million degree hot-thrust force, and will become our next generation of rocket engines. They use a few molecules of argon for fuel, then super microwave it to outrageous temperatures, and force it out the back nozzle of a magnetic bottle, to generate enough thrust to carry a huge ship all the way to Mars in only four months, instead of the previous fourteen month journey. The fuel is so efficient that the rockets can carry enough for a round trip out to Saturn!" The scientist smiled at the surprised expression his comments had shaped upon the face of his brother.

"Well, that would be great, and quite an honor, so I hope we can. It is astonishing just how rapidly our technological advances are accelerating, now in these last years!" The archeologist slightly shook his head, as he recalled all that had occurred within the last ten years.

"Yes, it really is. Well, He did say that many would rush to and fro, and also that knowledge would be increased much, in the last days."

The archeologist replied, "That's true, and it is evidently happening right before our very eyes! I suspect the increase in knowledge is a sort of final crop from the Tree of Knowledge. Perhaps God is allowing mankind's knowledge to be opened to this extraordinary extent, for the express purpose of proving, once and for all time, that knowledge alone, no matter how great, will never be sufficient to handle everything. God's grace will always be sufficient, but mankind's wisdom is still too foolish in this present, darkened age to enable correct decisions. We need more of God's wisdom, instead."

"Wisdom seems to be essentially learning to see and do things God's Way, instead of ours."

The archeologist barked a delighted sharp laugh, and said, "Well said, little Brother! You just won the 64-dollar question!"

The scientist smiled, then answered, "Yeah, well, that's why they keep promising to pay me the big bucks. I better get it right. We don't get any second chances out there in space, and AAA does not yet have tow trucks that can get that far. Come on. Let's head to the house. Rebecca and the kids are chomping at the bit to see you again. Tomorrow, after we go see Franklin, and his new rockets, we will stop by the moon museum for a few minutes, and I want to show you some of the new things which they put in recently."

As they stood up and stretched, the scientist tossed a little, sealed, shatter-proof vial over to him, and said, "You remember that Neil Armstrong ad-libbed an additional task into the mission outline, once he was standing upon the moon. He used his little scoop shovel to pick up some of the lunar top soil, which is called 'regolith'. That is a small sample of it. Don't open the vial, please."

As the archeologist held in his hands a relic from another world, his pulse began to race, and his heartbeat thundered in his ears. He calmed his breathing, and slowed his heart a bit, and then asked, "The real thing?"

His younger brother chuckled, and said, "Of course! The stuff in that vial is why we're all going to go back to the moon, to stay, this time!"

The older brother asked, "Why?"

"Because we found out that it contains some stuff called helium-3, which is non-existent upon Earth, since it is only produced by the intense solar wind, and cannot reach the surface of the Earth, because of the atmosphere, and the magnetic shield, but it impacts and becomes imbedded into the moon's surface material, or lunar soil, or 'regolith'. It is like hard-packed little brittle pieces, small chunks of lava and glass, with a sandstone-like behavior, but it can be broken up and pulverized, and then processed for the treasure which it contains. What it can do is allow us to produce genuine cold fusion, with no radiation, no extra heat, and pure, limitless electric current, so easily and cheaply produced that a passenger car could use it to drive for years on a single fuel-up. We could fuel the entire U.S. for a year, vehicles and cities alike, with about 200 pounds of it!"

"Wow. So why are we not already up there loading it into space trucks to bring home?"

"Well, the stuff is troublesome to mine, even though it covers the entire surface, in all of the dust. The concentration is so sparse, that it takes about a football field's worth of regolith to mine out a few pounds of helium-3. That takes time, and machinery, and manpower to run the machinery, or to fix the robots which run the machinery."

"Obviously, that's why the need for a long-term base arose, but what about food, water, and fuel? Even if the helium-3 is already there, how soon can it be harnessed to use there on the lunar surface?"

"You are quite correct, big Brother! So, what we are doing about those things is a lot of solar power, with some small nuclear to take over, when during the night cycle. The real vital need is water: to drink, and to cook, and to shower, and to do laundry. Also, air will be at a premium. Water has oxygen, and the components of water, hydrogen and oxygen, can be re-used as rocket fuel, which is the same type of rocket fuel used by the Space Shuttle boosters."

"I guess that means that you are first hunting for buried ice, under the lunar surface, where sunlight can't evaporate it?"

"Yes. Man, it's easy to explain things to a person that catches on quickly! What a delight!"

"So, that must require a deep crater, or canyon, maybe near the poles?"

"Right, you are! As it seemed good in the sight of our good Lord, He just happened to create such a place, at the very south pole of the moon. It is called Shakleton Crater, and we think we can find some ice down at the bottom of it. That's the new target zone, ground zero, for the new, hot space race. Every nation, and his dog, is busting a hump to get there first, and build a permanent base, and begin mining helium-3."

"But I thought that the helium-3 came from the intense sunlight, and the solar wind, and how then does that get to the polar region? Does enough intense sunlight fall there?"

"No, it does not, but we still need to start there, to get the needed ice. We must have the ice machine, before we can start the party."

As the archeologist handed back the vial, his brother gave him a rock, and said, "Now that's a real moon rock, one of about 845 pounds of them dragged back here by the six Apollo missions. You can see that it is not made of green cheese."

The split second that the archeologist felt the moon rock touch his skin, he suddenly was somewhere very different. He was looking out the view from inside a space suit, and could feel the stiffness of the rest of the suit all over his body. He looked up, and saw unlimited stars, blazing like little white lasers, dazzlingly intense, and steady, with no blinking. He looked down, and saw only solid black, and no stars at all. He could not find anything at all in the ocean of darkness before him, and began to feel a growing panic, when his eyes could not find any anchor for visual focus. He looked back up at the stunning stars, and breathed deeply, slowly, until his heartbeat slowed down some, and then, with a whispered prayer, began to cautiously lower his gaze again, toward the emptiness below. He was not feeling weightless, but feathery light, like a strong breeze could carry him away. He realized he had instinctively hunched into a crouched position, being unsure what might be coming next. As his sight began to adjust, he began to notice some sort of dim gray line in the far distance, running horizontally all across his field of view. His eyes followed it around to the right, and it kept going, becoming more visible over time. It seemed like the further to the right his eyes tracked, the brighter and thicker the line was becoming. He continued to track the line around to the right, noting that it was about perfectly horizontal, or what seemed like flatly horizontal, with no up or down slope to it. Ultimately, when he was facing relative due east, turned to his extreme right, his eyes followed the line right up to the boots of his space suit! He instantly realized that he was standing upon the very rim of something overwhelmingly huge, and black, and empty. He reflexively jumped back away from the edge a few feet, and dropped to his belly, clutching at the rock beneath him.

Whatever that hole was, he did NOT want to fall into it, feather-light body, or not.

His heart raced, and his pulse pounded in his ears, and his breathing rasped rough and ragged inside the space suit.

He suddenly heard a hearty laugh right in his helmet speakers, and a strong male voice boomed in his helmet, "All right! I haven't seen anyone do that reaction since I did it, just like that, about a month ago! Way to go, Rookie!"

He turned his face to the side, and saw another man standing there next to him, bending down near his face. As he looked into the faceplate of the other suit, he saw a flash of white teeth, and a pair of dancing blue eyes, and heard the ongoing booming laughter of the other astronaut. He also began to notice other voices laughing in the helmet speakers, and heard other astronauts joining in the fun, at his own embarrassing condition. Cautiously, he began to stand up, and look over the edge again, wondering if he had maybe over-reacted.

Nope. Infinite, empty, even void of stars, and beyond the grasp of normal human comprehension, the darkness was truly terrifying, at least until a person had a chance to become adapted to it, and even the veterans still felt a shiver in their bones when they first saw it, every time. (Such a thing did not even seem to belong anywhere in a sane universe, at least not anywhere around humans.)

"It's okay, you get used to it, sort of. No one's been down inside there yet, except for some recon robots and drones. It is spooky, all right."

The archeologist realized that he was experiencing another vision, but this time it was a view of future events, not past. Apparently, he was indeed upon the moon, standing at the rim of what he guessed was Shakleton Crater. Imagine a hole huge enough to set the entire city of Dallas, Texas down flat at the bottom of it, and still have enough room around the edges for a large loop freeway. Shakleton is over 12 miles across, which is well over half the maximum width of the Grand Canyon.

If there were two skyscrapers, each 500 stories tall, stacked on top of each other, there would still be enough room left to stack a modern aircraft carrier lengthwise on top of the two skyscrapers, and it still would not reach the height of the rim. The Grand Canyon is over a mile deep in places, but Shakleton Crater is over 2 and 1/4 miles deep.

The Grand Canyon has much terrain variation, having been carved out by flooding river waters, but Shakleton is mostly smooth, except for some huge boulders here and there, and some furrows and cracks in the relatively flat floor, although there is a hill in the very center. It is tiny compared to the rest of the crater, and was either formed, right after impact, by a shockwave kickback, or had happened while the moon still had some fluid magma inside it, billions of years past. A rupture that deep into the surface would allow deep magma a chance to vent. Even if the internal magma had already cooled, the solar-flare type heat produced by whatever mountain of rock had slammed into the moon would have easily been enough to vaporize some of the lunar rock, and melt enough of the crust material to cause the adjacent rocks to flow like volcanic lava. After a few million years, the rocks had all cooled down. They had grown solid again, now being heat and pressure forged, as well.

The rocks cooled down all the way to about 40 degrees above absolute zero, since sunlight never enters the crater. At the south pole of the moon, the sun's angle is so extreme that not even a single ray of sunlight can ever reach below a few yards down into the crater. The temperature inside the crater is therefore about 30 degrees colder than Pluto. It is the coldest spot in the entire Solar System. Any comet ice down inside the crater will stay frozen, until mankind goes down into the crater, and brings it out, to obtain liquid water, and also oxygen.

So far, no one has been brave enough to actually want to go all the way down into the darkest and coldest place ever known to man. These astronauts would use robot machines, especially designed to function in the extreme cold. The robots would all carry their own nuclear power plants onboard themselves, since no battery could produce current at such temperatures. No one had yet designed or built a spacesuit that could endure such cold for longer than a short time, either. Even the material of the suit would begin to degrade, under such stress.

All of the electronics used in the special machinery would be made from the next generation of electronics materials, such as graphene, and fiber optic cables. Transistors could not function at those temperatures any better than batteries, since their materials could not pass electrons, when frozen to that extreme. Graphene and fiber optic cable did not need heat to work, just light, or current, depending. Super computers were helping to design all the circuits and programs that would be used, while human geniuses like the archeologist's brother were making the materials stronger and less brittle at super cold temps, so that they would not freeze and shatter, inside the crater.

All of a sudden, the helmet speakers crackled with the Commander's voice, and he said, "Okay, you two, get that camera set up, and the range laser, and get back here. Next incoming ship is due in the 'morning', and we need all hands here, at base, to off-load. Robinson, you and Blackberry step lively, but remain careful. If you fall in, we have no way yet to come down there and bring you back!"

The other man chuckled, and answered, "Aye, aye, Sir! Careful it is, even if my life insurance is paid up!"

The man nudged the archeologist with his space-suited elbow, and said, "Come on, Blackberry, you heard the Commander. Hand me that laser. I think that I have the mounting base clamped down tight."

The archeologist stood carefully up, being very sure to keep his balance, and he looked away from the black pit, to the man next to him, and said, "My name's not Blackberry."

Instantly, he was back in his brother's office, blinking at the sudden glare of normal office lighting. He realized that he was standing in a crouch, tightly gripping the moon rock with both hands, so hard that his knuckles were white, and his fingers hurt, and he had even slightly punctured his palms from pressure against the rock's rough spots. His brother was staring at him, jaw open, eyes wide with wonder, and a faint hint of a smile began to form as his composure returned, and the scientist asked, "What did you just say? Your name's not Blackberry? It happened again, didn't it?" He began to quiver with excitement, as he stared for answers into his older brother's eyes.

The archeologist returned the rock, swallowed, cleared his throat, asked for a sip of water, and received a plastic water bottle, and then opened it, and then said, after a couple of drinks, "Yes, I said that my name's not Blackberry."

His brother asked, eagerly, "What else? What else? What else?"

The archeologist answered, "Well, as soon as I touched that rock, I found myself in a space suit, on the moon, at the rim of Shakleton Crater! Scary. Anyway, as I was trying not to soil the space suit, for fear of that huge abyss, I noticed that I was there with another astronaut, a guy named Robinson."

At this, the younger brother leapt up, raced around his desk, grabbed his older brother by the shoulders, looked intensely deep into his eyes, and asked, in a hoarse whisper, "Robinson?" A few seconds later, he also whispered, more deep in thought, "And Blackberry, too! Huh. Strange."

The older brother went on, "That was not all that seemed odd. I would have expected Airforce fighter pilots to be the ones sent on a moon mission, as the best trained for flying, but the Base Commander was Navy, I think, since Robinson replied 'Aye, aye, Sir!' to the Commander, instead of 'Roger!'."

The younger brother asked, "Did anybody mention what year it was?"

The older brother thought a moment, then said, "No, I don't think so." Then he went on, "Why are you getting so fired-up? What does all of that mean to you?"

The younger brother looked at him for a couple of moments, thoughtfully, and then leaned over to his intercom, and told his receptionist to hold all calls and visitors, until he had finished up a private conference with his older brother. Then the younger one cleared his own throat, took a sip of water, and said, "Well, this is classified, but I think our good Lord has already apparently granted you a special universal security clearance, and is already revealing unto you things that few, if any, other humans are privileged to experience, so, if He wants you to know about these things, no one could stop it, anyway."

His brother took another sip of water, and then began, "The pieces of the vision which you told me convinced me immediately that it was a genuine future vision from King Jesus Christ. The names, the location, and even the branch of the military, against all odds, were precisely correct."

"The two men are two very Top Secret Special Operations Seal Team U.S. Navy Pilots, combat veterans, and fighter jet experienced, and each one of them is a confirmed ace with several air-to-air dogfight kills. Not all conflicts are revealed to public eyes and ears."

"All of the men on that particular team were hand picked, as the bravest, smartest, toughest, most original, and most creative problem solvers. They are the very best of the very best, and they have proven themselves as the elite ultra-soldiers and pilots which are required for this assignment. Also, being absolutely dedicated career military men, they are all single, with no children. They are 'spies without tails'. They cannot be pressured by any threat against their loved ones."

"The mission to Shakleton Crater is hopefully scheduled for sometime late in 2013, or maybe 2014. Five kilometers from the rim of the crater is what they have misnamed 'The Peak of Eternal Light', because it actually does remain in sunlight all but a few days in a lunar year. That will be the location for the permanent base which we will build there with inflatable domes, which will be solidified with hard coatings to provide durability. The well-lit 'Peak' is good for a landing zone, since one does not ever want to land upon the moon, or any other strange planet, except in sunlight. Even mostly flat terrain can have huge boulders in the way."

The older brother sighed, then said, "I wonder what this particular vision means, or what I am supposed to do with it. It's one thing if it is to strengthen someone's faith, but, actually, your faith and mine are blessed to be very strong. If it were to convert a non-believer, well, that would make sense, too. But all of this is Top Secret. We cannot use this vision, true as it is, to help anyone else, since we cannot tell them about it."

After a few seconds of intense thought, for both of them, the younger brother said, "I think I have it. Let's each write it down, and securely seal it, in our private, secret journals, or USB drives, or something like that, after we have each dated and locked the final write up. That way, later on, after the mission is already over, and successful, we can release these articles which we will write at this time. It will prove to be an excellent testimony, then, when it has come to pass, just as our good Lord has revealed it, through this vision!"

The older brother thought a second, and agreed. He said, "Well, there is not much more we could legally do with it at this time, anyway, without violating security protocols. We will write our personal, precise accounts, seal them, and give each other the only second certified copies. Each of us will have one copy each of both accounts, which will tell the same true facts."

"That way, we are doing these things according to our Lord's Way, as when He said that He would tell us before it came to pass, so that when it did come to pass, we would believe!"

The younger brother replied, "Yes, we do both already believe, but it may help someone else, a few years from now, after we can publish it, and they might also begin to believe, too! That's the whole point of what we're doing, or supposed to be doing, in this lifetime, anyway."

T MINUS 6

Most of the world already has forgotten, if they ever even noticed. The anniversary came and went quietly, and only a few people gave any thought, or pondered the unstoppable force of time marching forward, relentless, until it has finished working out God's purpose, as designed by God.

A year before, the winter solstice lunar eclipse occurred, and four days later, the largest gamma ray burst ever yet detected also showed up at Earth. Scientists still, a year later, are at a loss to accurately describe the precise cause of the monster burst, usually of the type produced when two large black holes merge, explosively. That one in December, 2010, has made all the run of the mill supernovae throughout the rest of the universe seem like little firecrackers, by comparison.

Precisely 90 days after the lunar eclipse (an event of a type so extremely rare that it happens only once, approximately, every 380 years), the sky event known as the "Super Moon", more accurately called the Perigee Moon, also was revealed, on March 19th, 2011. A few days before that, a huge earthquake hit Japan. In the weeks between the lunar eclipse, and the Super Moon, the first wave of revolutions started in the pattern now called the Muslim Spring, and many people have lost lives in the last year, because of it. Much bloodshed and strife are still now happening, in many of those same countries, and other new conflicts have also arisen.

Heads of states have died, or been removed from power, or both, and many new, untested players are appearing as world actors. Some of the same old fellows are still at it, too, such as Putin, in Russia, where his antics in rigging the last election have caused street protests.

(In olden days, such protests could never have happened.)

The U.S. finally removed its' military from Iraq, after a decade of wasted lives, time, and money down the drain, with nothing to show much for it, at all, except for a lot of bad will generated in the entire Middle East, toward the U.S. and Israel. (Ah, well, they already hated us, anyway.)

The U.S. has to learn the same lesson which the Russians had to learn, and which Alexander the Great had to learn centuries before. Persia, either ancient, or modern, is not only covered by a lot of sand, it is also quicksand, for any invading army. The U.S. can be slow to accept these lessons, as in both Viet Nam, and Iraq, and now it seems intent upon trying to repeat the same mistake, precisely the same way, in another section of Persia: Afghanistan. Too bad that the guys in uniform never get a vote where they shed their own blood.

All right, then, that brings us to one year down the road from a whole bunch of very strange and mysterious Heavenly signals and signs. There have also been many strange and unique signs and signals in the Earth. There are written warnings for us to beware of signs and signals in Heaven above, and the Earth beneath. All right, I will be watching, and perhaps every one else might find it of benefit, also. If truly enormous events are about to unfold, and world-changing phenomena are now beginning to occur, I want to be as ready as possible.

Even if I can do nothing to affect the outcome, of any particular event, or situation, except to pray, at least I want to know what I need to be praying about. What is beyond me is a small thing for King Jesus Christ. He might see fit to help, if we ask Him.

One thing I have noticed during a lifetime of prayer is this: it is wiser, to not wait to start praying until the last possible second. Maybe you miscounted the seconds. Better results can be obtained, if we start praying right now, before the storm even really can be seen forming.

The storm really is forming. You can smell it in the air. You can feel it in your bones. Our good Lord has already begun having His mighty angels start to pour out the first vials of wrath upon the Earth. There are more to come.

The sheep of the Good Shepherd know His Voice, and will not follow the voice of a stranger. For some of us sheep, it already makes our skin crawl, and chills our bone marrow, when we hear, upon rare occasions (so far), the voice of the anti Christ. We are listening for the Voice of King Jesus Christ, not a stranger.

SEVEN FLAMING SWORDS

Their appearances in Scripture are rare, but over-whelming. They each one correspond directly unto the Seven Gifts of the Holy Spirit. Another perspective in this matter also mentions the seven-fold Spirit of God, which is the original pattern of seven, from which all other patterns of seven proceed. In the vision of the Revelation unto John, they are described as the seven candlesticks before the Throne of God. Later in Revelation, they are revealed as the seven mighty angels having seven vials, full of the wrath of God.

In Isaiah, they are called the seraphim, and are described in more detail. They usually stand at attention, during special events in Heaven, as the honor guard, on top of the rainbow which encases the Throne of the Living God, and He glows too bright to see, with a blazing golden light, and appears like living flame. The seraphs also appear as living fire. They each wear six wings. Two wings fly, two more frame each face, and two more trail from the ankles. In appearance, they are like unto men, but dazzling in power and glory.

When they speak, Earthquakes happen. When they praise Almighty God, fire and smoke erupt out of their holy mouths. They are the special Judgment Executives for Almighty God. They can perform precise, surgical-type strikes, or blitz entire nations, or continents.

Their main wings are the grand ones, with which they fly, and those wings glow a stunning, bright, pure blue. The smaller wings at the temples are an electric crimson, a red so strong that it makes one gasp to see it. At the ankles are medium-sized, laser-green wings. The Name of the Father corresponds to the main wings, and the Authority of the Son of God corresponds to the wings beside the eyes, and the Power of the Holy Spirit corresponds to the wings at the ankles. Their faces glow a brilliant golden sunrise, which is impossible to watch, and their bodies ripple with the three primary colors, blue, red, and green, plus dazzling gold, also. The colors change intensity and pattern, reminiscent of the cuddle fish, depending upon the present action or emotion of the seraph. Whenever the seraph is angry, or rejoicing, the color patterns and displays are both thrilling and terrifying. Usually they are calm and serene, but not so during these last years of warfare upon Earth.

Earth, and its' total population, including humans, animals, fish, birds, bacteria, viruses, and whatever else lives within the Earth (including even the trespassing evil spirits, which are infesting regions of the Earth), are the particular jurisdiction of these ultra-cops. When Almighty God finally gives up on someone, or some nation, and says, "That's enough! Kill them, now!" it is usually the seraphs that handle it.

There are exceptions. Once, the General of the Angels, Tzedek-el, performed an execution mission upon 180,000 human enemies of Israel, in a single hour, at the specific orders of King Jesus Christ. Most of the time, things were done a different way. That mission had only been to destroy evil humans, and no animals whatsoever had been harmed.

When the seraphs acted, entire continents underwent changes, and oftentimes those changes even extended globally. Angels handled the more localized conflicts, while seraphs handled the monster issues.

Cherubs are exceedingly more powerful, still, than even the mighty seraphs, but seldom are sent to act, against anything or anyone, except the devil, which was once a cherub, also.

(The good cherubs always enjoy a chance to pound the enemy for a few minutes. Any longer than that could do virtually permanent damage, to the worm, and that is not allowed, until the Fire of the Second Death, after the Great White Throne Judgment.)

Since the three remaining good cherubs each govern a fundamental structural support of reality (namely: energy, time, and space), there is most often no real reason to order them to exert their powers, and doing so has to be performed most precisely, since changing a thing like time, or space, or the types and levels of energy in which the human race is immersed, can easily produce catastrophic results, if done recklessly. The worm once governed matter, but had his office stripped from him, and his power greatly reduced, after he sinned. King Jesus took over total control of matter, the day that He kicked the devil out of the Garden, and that prevented the devil from tearing apart the atoms of the Earth.

The seraphs have their authority limited to living creatures, and to the parts of the Earth environment which might be required, to obtain the ordered result, which is commanded by King Jesus Christ. The seraphs, like the cherubs, take orders only from King Jesus Christ, and no one else, since He is God!

Standing upon the viewing porch of the Palace, and looking down over the edge to the Earth, were King Jesus Christ, and Gabriel (the Cherub of Time), and Logos (the Seraph of Prophecy), and Tzedeka (the Seraph of Mercy), as well as General Tzedek-el (the General of the Angels), and Joshua (the General of Israel). They all stood silently watching the horrific bloodshed all over the whole Earth. After a few minutes, during which the anger and outrage grew and grew, stronger and stronger, in each one of their hearts, King Jesus cleared His throat, and said, "There will come the Day, soon, that great and notable Day of the Lord. On that Day, each one of you will fulfill his appointed mission perfectly, and I will also complete My Own mission that Day. Mercy will be granted unto Israel, and I will rescue them from the enemy, forever, and will return to save the remains of Israel, and also, all of the millions of true Christians still witnessing to the Truth about Me, fighting and dying for the Gospel, all during the Great Tribulation. As those of My brothers and sisters which fought and died for Me, during the First Century, won, and shall be evermore honored, so will My modern brothers and sisters win much honor by their own tough loyalty and valor, even unto miserable deaths, for My Name's sake."

He went on, "They do not have long to wait. We have now already crossed into the sixth year before I return. Seraphs, go now, and prepare, each one of you, all seven of your vials. The time is at hand, and I will soon command you to begin to pour out your vials upon the Earth!"

THE VOICE OF A STRANGER

The archeologist was staying overnight at his brother's house, in their guest room. After the amazing visions and experiences of the previous two days, the two brothers had had to schedule in an extra day, just to compare notes, and share insights, and information, and revelation. Both men understood that science was provably real, but the Holy Word of Almighty God was even more provably real, and infinitely more accurate, since science could not exist without the Word of God as its' foundational structure. If nothing had been created by the Word of God, science would not have anything to study, and would not exist itself, since humans would not exist, either!

The archeologist finished brushing his teeth, mouthwash following, and ran a comb once or twice through his still-drying hair, as he half-way overheard the audio from the television in the bedroom, which was the morning news headlines. He was thinking about what else he had to complete here Stateside, before he returned to Israel. He vaguely heard the broadcaster talking about the ongoing oppression in Syria by "Asad, the Animal", as the sub-human swine heartlessly, brutally massacred and tortured his own population. He half-heard the announcer say something about how this was all of great concern to Syria's neighbor to the south, Jordan. Abdullah of Jordan was sitting on his own powder keg, since only 30% of the population of Jordan was actually Arabian, like himself and the other Hashimites, the tribe of the descendents of the original followers of Mohammed, the madman. Abdullah was the only adult male now that was actually the direct blood-line descendent of Mohammed, from father to son, and he would soon be revealed as more than he seemed.

Suddenly, he froze, his eyes going slightly out of focus, for a split second, and his hands suddenly gripping the edge of the cabinet with a white-knuckled intensity, while the hackles on the back of his neck popped out like static lifted them. He felt a deep, deadly chill, far down in his soul, and the re-born spirit within him instantly rose up into combat against the terror, and squashed it into oblivion. Everything instantly cleared and calmed, and he whispered, "Yeshua!"

The voice which had triggered that reaction within him had been the voice of Abdullah of Jordan. As he walked out from the open bathroom door back into the guest room, and picked up the remote, and muted the sound (since the story had already moved on to other topics), he wondered deeply about those reactions, in his heart and spirit. What could that mean?

At that moment, his brother appeared at the bedroom door, knocked lightly on the frame, smiled, and said, "Morning! Want some breakfast?"

The older brother smiled, and said, "Yes, thanks, and morning to you, too! But first, I think something important just happened."

The younger sibling suddenly was all serious, knowing instantly that this was serious business. He asked, "Did you have another dream last night, or a vision this morning?"

The brother answered, "Not quite. When I heard the voice of someone on TV it gave me the chills, is all."

The scientist looked deep into his older brother's eyes, and asked, "Was it Abdullah of Jordan, just now?"

This time, it was the older brother that was stunned, and he answered, "Yes! How did you guess?"

The scientist replied, "We have it on in the kitchen, too. I just felt a deep chill, way down inside my soul, when I heard him talk, and I wasn't even looking at the screen."

Both men fell silent, lost in deep, intense thought. After a couple of minutes, the archeologist said, "I think that we need to pray right now. We need wisdom and courage, to deal with this thing which God has made known to us. Such a thing could not randomly happen like that to both of us, at the precise same moment, the precise same way. Unless I am very much mistaken, we have just been clearly told the identity of the anti-Christ!"

THE SEVENTH COMBAT MEDIUM

Military strategists plan operations to engage or elude the enemy by consideration of "just how to get there, from here". The distance between opposing armies must be crossed somehow, to deliver effective damage to enemy installations, equipment, positions, or personnel.

As far as human conflicts have gone, the first combat medium is Earth. One way to attack an enemy is to walk or run over to him and strike. (Or, maybe throwing a rock at him will do.)

The second combat medium is Sea. If a nation can move enough firepower around the entire world by ocean, the extent of their effective military presence is truly global. A lot of men, and missiles, and other weapons, like monster-sized naval guns, can be moved almost anywhere, in very little time, especially with modern nuclear-powered sea-craft. Many wars have been decided by naval actions.

The third combat medium is Air. Much of the credit for the Allied victories in World War II can be accounted to the mighty Allied airplanes, which kept delivering bullets and bombs against the Axis, until they beat them into surrender. People as manic as the Axis would never listen to reason, unless it was either surrender, or die.

With the second half of the 20th Century, the fourth combat medium began to be explored, when Sputnik was launched by the Russians, in October 1958. President Ronald Reagan understood this concept, and let the whole world know that the U.S. had begun research and development in the direction of the "High Frontier", also called "Star Wars", and which was actually designated the "Strategic

Defense Initiative", or S.D.I. The Russians knew they could not compete against that strategy, as the brilliant William Casey out-spent the Russians into military bankruptcy, and thereby collapsed the entire Russian economy. It was parasitic by nature, always surviving by exploiting the resources of its' occupied slave states, called "satellites", of course. Not long after those events, the Berlin Wall came down, and eventually there ceased to be the old Soviet Union.

It was not until the fiendishly clever rise of Putin that the old ghost of imperialistic Russia began to rear its' ugly, face-on-both-sides, cannibalistic head again. Putin was cagey enough to study the mistakes which were made by the preceding rulers of Russia. For one thing, he shrewdly avoided making overtly aggressive moves with the Russian army. After the debacles in Afghanistan and Chechnya, he knew not to even suppress the street protests against his government, and the rigged elections which he had tried to hijack, until he was caught, "red" handed! (Whether he won the election recount or not, it would be a long time before Putin would be removed from power. He had to stay around long enough to go help fight against Israel, when the dark alliance finally surrounded it.)

A certain feature of the different combat media helps to explain why they are ranked in the order in which they appear. It also helps illustrate why wars are won or lost by weapons launched from the higher medium against the lower. The mobility and gravitational leverage advantages almost always belong to the medium with the higher position.

To further illustrate, a ship with huge guns can fire exploding shells as far as 20 or even 30 miles inland, and yet change its' own position continually, even varying speed and course. The ship becomes a deadly launcher against fixed-location land targets, but it is a difficult ship to hit, because it is always moving around in unpredictable patterns.

What about air power? Along comes a bomber moving much faster than the ship, and up too high in the air for the ship's guns to reach it. A few big bombs later, and the burning ship begins to sink, while the plane flies happily home to get some more new bombs.

A bit farther into the modern era, and that plane is out hunting for more ships to sink, and then suddenly, with no warning at all, a laser beam spears down from a hunter-killer satellite, cutting deep into and through the cross section of the plane, dividing it into two separate pieces, front and rear, which both continue flying together for a few more seconds, but begin to slightly part, and then rip apart into flaming shrapnel, as the bombs and fuel onboard the plane flash instantly into a white-hot eruption that spreads a visible shock-wave out through the air all around where the plane used to be.

The land weapons fight uphill against all the others, and lose. The space-based weapons fight downhill against all the others, and never lose. Stuff always rolls downhill, as they say.

So, if that is the case, one might conclude that the space-based weapons are completely immune to attack. Not so fast, because they have to survive space itself, which is full of all sorts of heavily destructive things like solar flares, and gamma-ray bursts, and meteorites zipping along like rail-gun slugs, traveling sometimes as fast as a small fraction of the speed of light (if they were shot toward Earth by something like a supernova, shredding apart its' own planets, in its' death-flare). With no atmosphere to drag those little rocks to a stop, such interstellar buckshot could travel for billions of years, and then slam into a vital satellite one day. It might just punch a small hole, or it might blast the satellite into flames. All of the other combat media below orbit are shielded by our tough little atmosphere.

Now, as we enter the 21st Century, another combat medium is emerging as capable of launching weapons which are able to effectively work destruction against all of the previous combat mediums. Even satellites are not immune to cyber-attacks. Computer warfare is rapidly becoming the primary weapon of choice for doing really major damage to an enemy. Skilled agents can steal information, plant false information, erase true information, corrupt entire systems, or entire networks, and perhaps even the entire internet itself, all at once. Power grids can be shut off, or disabled permanently. Valves can be remotely opened or closed.

Communications systems and networks can be ruined. Control systems can be ruined or compromised, or entirely hijacked by agents, and turned against their own masters. Command capabilities are also vulnerable, since no general can get his orders to his troops, or find out if he should maybe change them, as needed.

Some differences do appear between this fifth combat medium, and the physical, geographic levels. Cyber-space is a virtual reality, not an actual place, or zone, and only exists because of the computer networks that operate it and prop it up with its' artificial existence, and its' phony reality. The one virtue, attribute, or commodity which is available through cyber-space is information exchange, between remote locations, systems, and operators. If the human race actually possessed telepathy, computer networks would not exist, except for machinery control.

Cyber-space-based weapons are still vulnerable to other cyber-space-based weapons and counter measures, also. An anti-virus program can kill a virus. A security encryption program can defeat most hackers. Recently, many U.S. companies, and also many governmental agencies have been deliberately attacked by foreign powers, among them China, most aggressively, and also Russia, probing for chinks in the armor. (The attacks were supposedly stopped before they did any real damage, or so they claim.)

Are there any other combat areas, or levels, or arenas which apply to life and death upon modern Earth, especially as relates to humanity? What about the area of the soul, which is defined, by King Jesus Christ, as composed of the heart, and the mind?

(Some people claim that the soul consists of the mind, the will, and the emotions, but that is not what King Jesus Christ said about it. He said that the heart produces all things: thoughts, words, and deeds, as well as plans and schemes. One thing which proceeds out of the heart is the will itself: what a person chooses to believe, or obey. This is essentially what the person wants to love. We are commanded to choose the fear of the Lord.)

To fulfill the desire of their heart, people set their will to perform, or accomplish, or experience some particular goal, or dream. The will is also a product of the heart, and is not actually a separate component. The only two actual discreet components comprising a human soul are the heart, and the mind, just like King Jesus Christ told us. Even so, the will is what determines our eternal future, since God has declared "And on Earth: peace, toward men of good will!"

Within the mind and heart there are continual conflicts at work. The selfish desires of all people war against the will to do good unto others, even at cost to oneself. The desire to remain responsible fights against the temptation to just chuck it all away. The desire to be in a close relationship with others is offset by the strife close relationships can often generate. The wish to co-ordinate with other folks is in conflict with the drive to act independently, without a conference-call first.

This is the region in which conventional weapons and attacks seldom seal the victory. True, if an enemy plane just dropped a bomb upon your personal home, it will do great damage to your heart and to your mind, even if you are out of town on vacation when it happens. Nonetheless, such a physical attack is not required, and damage can be wrought by other means. Many things can cause severe depression, such as the terrible financial struggles in which many excellent, hard-working, noble people are finding themselves entrapped these days. Chronic pain can wreck a life. Loneliness can be crushing. Loss of a loved one can be devastating.

Enough stress can cause a myriad of physical health problems and troubles, including death. Sanity is sometimes a casualty of such gruesome conflicts, which are usually invisible wars fought within each person, alone, in the middle of the night, or during the bright warm afternoon. Next time someone asks, "How are you doing?" would you feel comfortable giving a strictly accurate, if somewhat embarrassing, or humiliating, answer to that ordinary question? (How are any of us really doing, after all?) Besides, is the person asking that question someone who has a right to know, or are they just nosy? Or, do they actually really care at all? Could they help any, if you did tell them?

So, a great invisible battlefield exists all over the world, wherever humans are, even if they are upon the moon. The devil wages war and makes attack after attack against the heart and mind of every human, but King Jesus Christ fights back even harder, and the devil keeps getting his butt kicked, again and again. It would look comical, if the contested issue were not the salvation or damnation of each and every individual person of the entire human race. A lot of truth and a lot of lies are told in the battlefield of the human soul. The battle is choosing correctly what to obey, and sticking with it.

All right, that completes the list of the first six arenas for combat and conflict, a thing we call a combat medium. Are there any more? The answer is yes! One final level remains to illustrate.

To look back for a moment at the Battle of the Garden of Eden, the devil fired the first shot in the War between Good, and evil. When he tempted Eve, he violated God's Law, and sentenced himself to death, in the Lake of Fire. This was the first aggressive act of sin, and it brought forth death.

The reason why the attack happened upon Earth is because the devil could never launch any attack at all, within the Realm of Heaven. Almighty God rules all of Heaven with absolute Power and Authority, and no evil thing can be done there. The devil was instantly locked out permanently from Heaven, the very moment that he tempted Eve. No evil thing will ever be allowed into Heaven. God will not tolerate it to happen.

The seventh and final combat medium is the Kingdom of Heaven, which actually saturates the whole universe, but is currently concealed, until the Age of Faith has finished producing the finished Sons and Daughters of Light. King Jesus Christ said that all Power and Authority in Heaven and Earth was given unto Him. God as Father told us that He fills Heaven and Earth. He literally saturates all that exists, except the evil spirits, in which He has nothing, and they have nothing at all in Him. He is presently allowing them to stay alive only long enough to expedite the conclusion of the Age of Faith, and then He will kill them permanently, in the Lake of Fire.

The Kingdom of Heaven always wins. Conflict is not allowed within its' borders. King Jesus Christ even came down here to Earth as a human, to extend the borders of the Kingdom of Heaven all the Way back down to Earth, for us. Now, since the Resurrection, it is not possible for the devil to win upon Earth any longer. King Jesus Christ has taken back the keys to everything, and He will rule over it all as He sees fit!

The Kingdom of Heaven has never lost a war, and it never will. The King of Heaven has never lost a fight, and He never will. When Moses and Elijah appeared with Him, and were talking with Him about the death which He was about to accomplish at Jerusalem, it was certainly not His Own death which He sought. He came to kill the entire realm of sin, and the work of the devil, and, ultimately, the devil itself. He came to kill all evil, forever, and He did it, too! It's just taking us a while to get it to finish dying.

If you shoot a huge, strong snake in the head, it will eventually die, but it may do a lot of destruction while it is thrashing around in its' death convulsions. Even if it goes on for a while, you still have to hold on to faith that it will one day finally be over.

Remember, the Kingdom of Heaven is by definition of terms wherever the King says that it is, since His Word cannot lie. When our King came to Earth, He brought His Kingdom with Him.

The Earth is no longer enemy territory. It has been re-conquered for us by King Jesus Christ, through the undefeatable seventh combat medium, and He is still the perfect-record, never-beaten, overwhelmingly victorious, Holy, Almighty, King of Warriors! Rejoice!

The War is over, and He has already won!

THINKING IN 3D

For human sight, the distance between the eyes, around 3 to 5 inches (depending upon the size of the person's head), allows precise depth perception out to a distance of about 3 to 6 feet (again, depending upon the distance between those eyes). When there are two different angles of perception, the composite of the two views is perceived as a three-dimensional space, and the objects within that near range are understood by the mind as solid, real objects, and the scale of size is clear and precise. A softball two feet in front of you on the table will look like it is 4 inches in diameter, and located at a distance of two feet. Your mind just sees and knows that it is seeing what is actually there, in its' true nature, without distortion.

A person with an eye patch sees in only two dimensions, and direct 3D depth perception is not actually possible, since only one perspective is available. That visual experience is more like a color flat screen monitor, everywhere they look. Because the human brain is astonishingly adept at re-configuring itself to process and present information feeds into meaningful images, many people with the use of only one eye adjust very well to the flat screen view of life, and make automatic mathematical links to the real-world 3D environment, and they seem to function well, anyway, once they learn how to gauge the distance when pouring the milk.

All 3D television sets operate on essentially the same principle. Two cameras shooting the same object at the same time from two different angles will render a 3D image of the solid object. When played back through a set capable of showing both video feed lines simultaneously, a 3D image can be viewed. At this stage of the technology,

3D glasses are still required for the full effect to reach the mind of the viewer. Perhaps, when laser holographic technology has been advanced to a sophisticated enough level, 3D without viewing glasses will be common, if the television sets can display holographic signals, and show them in 3D.

Another circumstance in which a second angle can be of immense value is in combat, when applying the tactic of getting an enemy target in a cross-fire. There, you are shooting at the enemy target from one angle, and your fellow soldier is firing away at the same target from another angle. It is difficult for the enemy to hide from both rifles at once. Also, if he returns fire at one, the other opens up on him.

Another application of the two-angle method of information gathering is observed in the marine mammals such as dolphins, and whales, and others which use acoustic ranging and imaging. They are able to perceive 3D images within their minds which show them the underwater topography, other marine animals, and, in some cases, even things within the fluid medium of the sea itself, such as "thermoclines" (hard boundaries to sound caused by sharp differences in thermal layers of seawater of different temperatures). Sound waves bounce off of sharply colder water layers, or else they may be turned suddenly to a deeper angle, depending upon which direction the sound waves are traveling.

The marine animals are not alone in these techniques. Bats are also experts in using sound as a navigation and ranging device, which allows them to fly around in total darkness inside rocky caves and forests of big trees, without hitting anything, even each other in flight, even in clouds of thousands of bats leaving caves at sundown, to hunt millions of mosquitoes all night long.

The primary difference is the sense organs, which are two eyes for sight, but two ears for sound. Still, we can personally know that the principle does hold true, since we humans also can hear and experience surround, 3D sound ourselves, and we know that it works perfectly well.

For those who are familiar with map and compass, the way to establish a precise current location for one's self is to shoot bearings on two known, fixed reference points, and then plot the intersection of the two sight lines. Where the lines cross is where you are.

Even the most advanced forms of 3D rendering, such as laser holograms, can usually only be achieved by splitting a single coherent laser beam into two equal and identical coherent beams, still in sync with each other, and striking the same target from two different angles, and then projecting, or recording, the resulting 3D image. (There are a few rare, complex, high-tech exceptions.)

The newest and most effective ground-based telescopes use a similar concept, combing the images from two or even more identical telescopes, set at a fixed distance apart from each other on the ground, and focused upon the same precise target, in the sky. The result is that of a telescope many times larger than the total size of all of the individual ones actually used, because of the optics, as they are here applied.

Even information exchange is compliant with this mode of operation. Whenever intelligence information is first detected, it is usually immediately the target of either confirmation, or denial. Only after a second observer, or spy, confirms the initial report, is any solid credibility awarded.

This principle is even clearly spelled out by our good Lord, King Jesus Christ, when He told us to bear testimony in the mouths of two or more witnesses, that every word may be established. It is recorded that He even helped to also bear Witness, when the Apostles preached the Gospel, with accompanying signs. He worked miracles, to prove the Truth.

This is the same two-angle approach which is used by some of us who seek to accurately perceive the deepest nature of Reality, as designed, built, and maintained by the Almighty Creator. Those of us which believe the Holy Word of God, as absolute Truth, and the foundational structure of all creation, seen and unseen, also can understand and appreciate the complex nature of scientific information, much of which is precisely accurate, and provably verifiable, by demonstration, or experiment.

This is not to say that everything science thinks it knows is correct. A few hundred years ago, the Earth was considered flat, and it was thought to be the center of the entire Universe, and there were not known to be such things as germs, and no one thought an atom could be split. "Doctors" did not even wash their hands with soap and water, until 150 years ago, not even the surgeons.

On the contrary, everything recorded in the Holy Word of God has always been correct, and true, and the more that "science" figures out, the more correct the information in the Word of God is proven to be. God said, "Let there be LIGHT!" Several billion years later, some creatures which God created out of dust finally figured out that there was a Big Bang, way, way back at the start of everything that exists, just like it always was recorded, accurately, in the Holy Word of God.

Nonetheless, modern science is very advanced, and nowhere that I have seen in the Scriptures can I learn that the huge central black hole at the core of the Andromeda Galaxy is at least 50 times the mass of the central black hole at the core of our own dear Milky Way Galaxy, or that in approximately 2 billion more years, our two very large galaxies will crash into and through each other, merging in huge, slow, motion into one even grander and more majestic galaxy, no matter how many stars must die along the way. Quite a show, if we could only hang around long enough to use our front row tickets!

This brings us to the core concept for this discussion. If we wish to perceive, as clearly as possible, the precise, hidden nature of all Reality, seen, and unseen, we must take a dual perspective approach to accurately understand and see the subject, in "3D" type, solid Reality. Our minds can combine the information feeds from what we can learn from the latest science (at least, the proven parts, not the wild and unsupportable nonsense like more than one universe, or "loop quantum gravity", or invisible, never-to-be-seen little "strings"), and the reliable, never disproved, or disprovable, Holy Scriptures, and we can learn to look for, ferret out, and sometimes clearly "see" the hidden nature of Creation, and also maybe catch a fleeting glimpse of the Creator, Himself.

As far as clearly perceiving the Almighty God which created everything, and everyone else, He has provided us with His Ways, so that we might seek Him, and know Him. He has made for us this astonishing physical Universe, way beyond anything which we will ever understand. (We cannot even correctly understand our own little planet.)

He has also generously given us His Holy Word, which will always remain an accurate source of precise Truth.

He has also given unto us, the re-born, His Holy Spirit, the Spirit of Truth, which will always be an unfailing source of Truth.

The greatest of all testimony and witness about Himself yet given unto us, or ever possible for Him to give unto us, is the Holy Begotten Son of God. The Scripture declares that no man has seen God at any time, but the Only Begotten Son of God has revealed the Father unto us. The Father and the Son indeed are the same Person.

The Father told us that King Jesus Christ is His Holy Son, and commanded us to hear King Jesus. King Jesus explained the Kingdom of Heaven unto us, and commanded us how to live out our lives as newly re-born citizens of the Kingdom of Heaven, even while we're still here upon Earth. King Jesus Christ also sent Himself, as the Holy Spirit, unto each of us, to help us to overcome, and to continue to hear, and to obey, and to follow His leadership, all the Way, His Way, Home to Heaven, and to Him!

So, if you want to "see" a more complete and precisely accurate view of the whole of Creation, seen and unseen, you must look at it from both angles: the supreme accuracy of Holy Scripture, and also the latest provable scientific information which we can discover in this 21st Century.

Pray also for our good Lord to help open up your deep understanding even further, and to escort you through the mysteries which He wishes to share with you. Be open-minded and flexible, and remember that with God, nothing shall be called impossible. No one but God knows all of the correct answers. All of the rest of us are still learning.

A person is known in this world by two main things, apart from the physical appearance and size. What a person says, and what a person does, is how we can tell what is inside that person. Our good Lord told us that we will know them by their fruits, since a good tree bears good fruit, but a bad tree bears bad fruit. He also told us that "as he thinks in his heart, so is he." Whatever is hidden inside a person's heart will reveal itself, since from the heart spring all manner of either good things, from a good heart, or evil things, from an evil heart. When a person's words and deeds are good, and the words and deeds match up, then we can tell that the person has solidity, and true-hearted good will.

Also, if you wish to know the Holy Scriptures more fully, then read, and obey. The more you obey, the more God will probably open up your deep understanding, if you stick with it.

Further, if you wish to know the Holy Spirit more fully, then hear, and obey. The more you follow His lead, and obey, the more He will certainly open up your deep understanding, through Him.

Do remember, and use a two-angle approach to the same target. That always gives you a better chance of an accurate view of the real nature and size of the thing considered. It also provides accurate distance, or range information.

Use the Scriptures, and allow yourself to be used by the Holy Spirit, and you will be applying the correct two-angle approach to "seeing" God. At the very least, you will have a steadily clearer vision of Him, and it will hopefully keep all of us looking in the right direction, which is toward Him!

WHEN THE MONSTER SNORES

The very thought of it had kept me impatiently eager, and it had been continuing for several weeks. Near the end of my second grade year, my wonderful parents told me that we were going to take a special vacation trip later in the summer. We were going to a mysterious and unique place, where bears and all sorts of other wild animals roamed free and unconfined, amidst rising spouts of hot water (geysers) and thick clouds of steam that puffed out of the ground itself, in various places. Any eight-year-old boy would thrill at such a journey, and I certainly did.

My Dad had only been with Bostitch for a few years, and the other men with more seniority got to choose the earlier vacation slots first. We did not get to head out on the road until August. We camped out all the way up there, since part of the fun was the outdoor environment, and it was plenty mild, even up in the Rockies, as long as you did not go up very high. All the way across Texas took a whole day.

That afternoon, we went past Rabbit Ear Mountain, as we cut across the corner of New Mexico, into Colorado.

Then, we found a campground at Estes Park, and spent a couple of hours fishing for supper in a stream. I tried using popcorn left over from the highway journey, and the trout liked that better than anything else! I caught the most fish of all of us. (They were delicious, too, and we didn't even notice the popcorn flavor.)

The next morning, we went on up to Pikes Peak, and drove up to the summit, and then continued on the journey north. I had been born in the mountains around Birmingham, Alabama, but it had been a long time (I was three years old, when we left) since I had seen any large ranges.

I was truly enjoying the whole experience, but I wonder if my Dad did it just to get to drive a lot of miles in his 1958 Thunderbird convertible. The trunk was just barely big enough for us to stuff in all of our camping gear and clothes, and I was just small enough to be able to ride in the little space behind the front seats, but it was definitely not a back seat. It was more of a shelf area, large enough for a small suitcase, or an eight-year-old boy. I would not have missed it for anything!

I did notice that Dad never would let Mom drive during the whole trip, even though she of course knew very well how to drive a standard shift. Every car she drove until she was forty years old only came with a standard transmission. That changed in 1951, when my Grandfather gave my parents a brand new Pontiac, so they could more safely drive the new baby over to visit his grandparents in Texas. (A couple of years later, we moved to Texas in that Pontiac.)

Finally, as the day began to wane, we arrived in Yellowstone Park, which had seemed (to me) like my own little "promised land", and we found the official campground. We unpacked to settle in, pitch the tent, inflate the air mattresses, build the campfire (in the little cooker fireplace they had made there for campers to use) and then cook, and eat, with thanks. We turned in pretty early, after a quick splash through the showers, and I do not remember any more at all until the next day.

Our first morning there, we woke up, made a quick little breakfast, and headed over to the main lodge, to find all the maps and tour information we could, so that we would know what was best to see, and how to get to it. Yellowstone is huge, and it takes a little planning to manage to see the most important sites and sights, and do it all in just a few precious days and nights. We only had two weeks to drive up there, see everything, and then drive home.

We gathered the free information booklets, and trail maps, and road maps which they offered, and we scanned over the displays and special notices about not feeding the bears, and staying on the little board walks, as well as staying behind the rails near all of the geysers, so we would not be boiled alive. We noted and took all of these dire warnings to heart. Neither in Alabama nor Texas had I ever seen bears or geysers, and I believed all of the serious warnings the brave park Rangers kept telling us. After all, they lived every day among those bears and geysers, and knew how to survive. (It seems odd, how none of them warned us about Earthquakes.)

We hopped back in our car, I mean, my Dad's cool little Thunderbird convertible, and off we went for several hours of driving from one point to another, inspecting bubbling mud puddles with a strong rotten-egg smell (from the concentrations of sulfur gas compounds released into the air nearby), and also seeing many geysers, although most of them were on longer cycles than Old Faithful, which has stayed on the same, stable "just-less-than-an-hour" schedule, ever since modern man has been keeping track of it. Some geysers were on cycles of every fourteen hours, or every four days, or every two months, or something else like that, and many were irregular in their timing, and were difficult to accurately predict. Those dangerous spouts were kept away from the public, since no one wanted to have a dozen tourists flash-boiled alive.

That night, we went back to the campground, made another wonderful cook out supper, and then, after some social visiting with our camping neighbors (folks were much more friendly back in 1959), we made sure the air mattresses were full again, and instantly lost awareness of the outside world, as soon as head met pillow.

The next day was still more scenic-overload type exploration, and a lot of photographs, and several Park Ranger learning lectures, about geysers, bears, bubbling mud puddles, and all sorts of other fascinating subjects. These lectures were presented by one or two Rangers at the sites, whenever a large enough crowd had gathered. The talks usually only lasted for five or ten minutes, but were very informative. It greatly enhanced the appreciation the visitors had for the things which we were seeing right in front of us. (I still think it odd, that none of those lectures mentioned anything at all about Earthquakes.)

As the day wound down, we returned to the campground. We fixed supper, showered, and crashed. I was absolutely exhausted. The perpetual scenic overload was very energy draining. If you have an eight year old boy which never seems to run down, take him up to Yellowstone for a week. By the third night, he will be very tame, due to discharged batteries.

The last thing I recall before unconsciousness was my Mom wishing us "pleasant dreams", and all of us saying "good night", and then, silence. I was so deep in sleep that I slept straight through a few very exciting minutes.

I woke up with exhausted difficulty, hearing the sound of adult voices, not too far away. Every few seconds, the grown-ups would erupt into happy laughter. I looked around our tent, but no one was in there except me. I grabbed my flashlight, like any well-trained Boy Scout, and leapt up to go out scouting.

I emerged from the tent, and looked toward the sound of the adult voices. It was a bright, moonlit night, and I could see a group of about a half dozen grown ups, all standing in the moonlight, laughing as though at a party, and telling funny things, which set them all off laughing again.

I walked cautiously over to them, and recognized my Dad and Mom among the folks there, and when a brief moment of silence happened, I asked what was going on. Dad and Mom turned and welcomed me, and explained that there had been an "Earthquake". I was not quite sure what that was, but asked if it was going to be all right. They assured me that everything was okay. In a sense I suppose that it was, indeed, since everyone there in the Yellowstone Campground was sleeping in tents, there were no major buildings to collapse and crush us!

The conversations continued, as did the laughter, and some other kids also woke up and came to see where their parents had gone. There were a few more adults there, too. Many had slept through the initial tremor, just like I did. Between the combination of extremely deep exhaustion, and a very pleasant summer climate, and a good, thick air mattress, even a 7.6 magnitude Earthquake had a tough time shaking some of us awake that night.

A few people had decided that a single tremor was one too many, and had struck camp immediately, throwing stuff into their cars excitedly by the moonlight. Some cars pulled out through the middle road of the campground, and we watched them drive by. All of the folks inside those cars had scared looking faces, with big, wide eyes staring out the windows.

Within 10 minutes, I experienced my second tremblor, and, just like all of the adults standing there in the moonlight, I instinctively flexed my knees, and lowered into a crouch, trying to keep my balance, as the ground decided to act like a gigantic trampoline under our feet. It only lasted for a minute or so, and then things returned to still. Everyone kind of smiled nervously, and then straightened up to full height again, and nervous laughter rang out again in the moonlight. My Mom was telling me that it was okay, and just to wait a minute, to see if it was done.

A few minutes later, everyone decided wisely just to turn back in, and wait until morning to survey for damage. We fell back asleep, although it was a bit difficult, no matter how tired we were.

The next morning, we went over to the Visitor Center, and were asking the Rangers that we saw outside the Lodge what the latest news might be. They told us about a brand new lake that had formed overnight, and that several of the geysers had apparently changed their timing cycles. One particular case was a geyser that had been known to fire every 14 days. Quite mysteriously, it changed its' timing to every 14 hours, a 24-fold increase. Many of the Park roads had been either ripped apart, or blocked by falling rocks. At one remote camp location, a serious landslide had happened, and some people were killed. That was one of the further areas which we had been planning to see before we left, but now, with the road blocked, and actual emergency rescue operations going on there, we would not be allowed to go there.

As we were talking with the Rangers, suddenly a low rumble growled from everywhere around us at once, and the pathway in front of the Visitor Center began to roll up and down, in waves, just like it had turned to water, and had suddenly become strapped to the surface of the ocean. The waves were not too big, only a foot or so tall, but we still had to crouch, and fight for balance, as our heartbeats all shot up again to outrageous levels. The wavy Earth settled back down instantly, less than a minute after starting, and we all watched and listened as several large chimney stones that had been loosened the night before came crashing and sliding down from the top of the Visitor Center Lodge. People shouted, and moved away rapidly, until all the movement stopped.

After enough of all of that aftershock stuff, my Dad and Mom said it was time to leave, so, we went back to camp, broke down the tent, loaded up everything, made some sandwiches for the road, gassed up the 1958 Thunderbird convertible, and headed back to Texas. We had been planning to also swing by the Grand Tetons, and Jackson, but had stayed on the fastest return route, instead. One day, I will return, and this time, I will also visit those sights, too.

It still amazes me that I was so very tired, that I slept through the initial, strongest shock, air mattress, or not. Even if that had not waked me up, one would expect the sudden response of my absolutely fearless Dad, who just happened to be a decorated WWII hero, would have likely awakened me. What my mighty Dad did was jump up, grab his flashlight, and leap over to the side of the tent where the shaking was the fiercest. His sleepy mind had switched on to full battle mode, and he thought that a bear was trying to tear through the tent to eat us! Undaunted by the threat of doing hand-to-hand combat with a 1,000-pound grizzly bear, my Dad had shouted, "Sooey, bear, sooey!" as he beat against the side of the tent with the flashlight. No grizzly, however hungry or tough, was ever going to get past my Dad when he was defending his family! (Of course, he took a bit of ribbing from his co-workers when we returned, and the story made the rounds. Dad said that he knew that bears were a part of the pig family of animals, and so he yelled at it just like any other big pig!)

I noticed a strange thing though, when I heard his friends teasing him a little about the "sooey" thing. Every single man that shared a chuckle with him about it did so with a subdued note of amazed respect in their voices. They realized that that level of raw courage is a very rare thing indeed. (They should have seen him in action on the P.T. boats.)

Dad was not the only mighty warrior in our family that night. My Dad showed the fearless courage to willingly engage a grizzly bear, or what he truly believed was a grizzly bear, but my Mom had the confident trust in our good Lord, and her husband, that she calmly kept me from freaking out during the whole thing.

I really was not all that scared. It was not easy to feel fear around those two. I think maybe that the only one that ever felt much fear around my parents was probably the devil. I think the thing knew that they were going to whip his butt, again and again, all the way through their wonderful lives!

As it turned out, I could have warned it about that. Even until I joined the Navy, my folks always could whip my butt, too, anytime they felt that it was needed! I still give thanks that such events were rare.

GOOD NEIGHBOR POLICY

Abdullah tossed restlessly in his dream. As his vision swept northward, he scanned quickly over the entire country of Syria, and the neighbors around. His view was rapidly zooming in to the headquarters of Asad, the butcher, but many instant, vivid flash-visions also showed him various places here and there where people were held in dungeons, and tortured, and raped, and mutilated, and murdered. This included any and all that were thought to be rebels against the insane dictator, and his demon-possessed mother.

Abdullah wanted to protect his own throne, also, but had found far less brutal ways to accomplish his goals. His nation did actually produce a fair amount of wealth, and a large portion of it came from the strategic location of being a part of the cross roads area of the Middle

East. Jordan connected to almost all the major countries in the region, including Syria, Israel, Iraq, and Arabia. Egypt, Iran, Turkey, Ethiopia, and Lebanon were no more than two countries away, also. All of the oil-kingdoms, and, also, coincidentally, almost all of the Islamic countries, except for Malaysia, Pakistan, Afghanistan, and Chechnya, were within a few hundred miles at most from Amman, and a lot of folks all around Jordan wanted to move certain things, including people, from one country to another, without being detected, or arousing suspicion, or some other sort of interference.

Of course, there were official border crossings, and some not-so-official ones, as well. Strange, how the highest officials (only) were the ones which knew about the unofficial border crossings. A lot of manpower and firepower had to be committed to keeping those hidden gateways operating, and hidden. That took money, and even if Jordan was not the richest of the oil countries, their neighbors were, and they were the customers which kept shipping all sorts of things through, unseen, unknown, year after year. The U.S. knew about a lot of it, but not all, and since Jordan was officially an "ally" in the "peace process", a lot of looking the other way had to be applied by the U.S., since calling Jordan out on it would sever the "ally" status, and further destabilize the region.

A nice inherent advantage to owning the crossroads is that you get to charge a toll. That toll can become outrageous, if the cargo or contraband being transferred is with secrecy required. Sometimes, the most valuable items were people, not machines or weapons. One thing all such hidden transactions produced was cash, and tons of it. Any ruler, such as Abdullah, with tons of cash, hidden cash, in an unlimited and endless supply, can, and does, buy the absolute loyalty of his people, using rewards, instead of bullets and tanks, to keep his ranks in line. Few rulers anywhere in the Middle East had the intense, lifetime adoration, which the people of Jordan showed to Abdullah.

The generous, and widespread, though unofficial, reward system was not the only motivation which kept the Jordanians loyal. They also knew that Abdullah was the Hashimite, the direct blood-line heir of Mohammed. He was the only person in the whole world with an inherited right to become the Caliph, and the Mahdi. A Christian would understand this as the concept that he was the one prophesied to become the "anti Christ". He is referred to as "the son of perdition". That nickname only applied to one other person, in all of human history: Judas Iscariot.

Abdullah had been western-educated, and trained especially in the fine art of high-level diplomacy by none other than his own father, King Hussein of Jordan. One of the advanced skills which had been honed to perfection was wearing the polite, smiling, soft-spoken mask of the negotiator, while all the time plotting a way to turn the trust of the opponent into a leverage against them in the future. The tactic was to agree to anything, just to extend the uneasy peace, long enough to strengthen one's own army, and then strike at a time in the future, once the enemy's alert level had dropped down enough.

As the view zoomed in through the walls, and came in close on Asad (as he walked up and down the halls of his palace, muttering things to himself), other flash-visions continued to fade in and out all the time, and more and more of them were showing the rebel forces and leaders, and then, many well-concealed crossing points, including many, many well-hidden tunnels. He saw a few futuristic type flash-visions of himself meeting with both CIA and Russian agents, but not at the same time, and making backstage deals, which somehow brought in more money and weaponry from both monster countries, and kept each side thinking that they had Abdullah right in their pockets, and so, in their puppet-strings. (Of course, it was obvious that the CIA wanted Asad gone, since he was a human rights pervert, but, he was also a heavy customer for Russian military hardware, and a pipeline for Iran's support of Hezbollah, in Gaza. The Russians did not care if it was Asad, or Abdullah and the Syrian rebels, whichever bought their AK-47's, just as long as they got paid in cash.)

The U.S. and Russia would never understand, until way too late, that every detail of it was part of his plan for years. (The puppet was the one pulling the strings just enough to keep the big boys a little off balance, all the time!) One day, when they were not expecting it, those little strings would prove to be like the cords used on Gulliver, but they would bind vital areas, and would tie up the monsters long enough for Abdullah to make his major strategic thrust, without the interference of either the U.S. or Russia. (At the end of it, he would be the iron-fisted ruler of over 80% of the oilfields of the Middle East.)

Meanwhile, the rebels needed a friend. The one that helped them to overthrow Asad was going to be able to insist that they would later follow him and his army into war, as required. If the rebels wanted help now, when they needed it, they would have to agree to help Abdullah, when he went to help the Egyptian rebels win their civil war later, in Egypt. The result would be that in three years, his own army would include the loyal armies from the victorious rebels in Syria, Egypt, Lebanon, Yemen, Somalia, Ethiopia, Malaysia, and Chechnya. Turkey would get in line, or be destroyed, as with Pakistan, nukes or not. Iran was officially playing the role of lightning rod, drawing away the focus of the West from where the real major hidden action was happening. This took a lot of courage and commitment from the Iranians, and they had already shown a strong, secret support for him, ever since the beginning. Somebody had to play the saber-rattler, and give the West something to distract them, while the real work was achieved slowly and carefully, out of Western sight.

He sighed, smiled a wicked little smile, and turned over on his side to drift back off into deep sleep. It was all textbook Muslim battle tactics, to first be a warm friend to your enemy, and then exploit that closeness at the right time. The same principle would work just as well, if one applied it to a growing Syrian rebel army. Those resistance fighters which got help from him now would be bound to fight for him one day against Israel. Before they took on Israel, the entire new monster army which he would glue together would follow him back down into Arabia. After killing the so-called royal family there, he would proclaim the land as restored to his family, in memory of his father, from whom it had been stolen. The Hashimite would once again rule Mecca and Medina! He would do it by deceitfully trading mercy now, in order to later force their service for himself.

After that, it would finally be time to move against Israel. All things were to be done in their proper time, and not one minute sooner. As he faded back into deep sleep, he thought he faintly heard the scary stone voice chuckling quietly, like a proud parent when his boy got a good grade on a test.

FIRE AND BRIMSTONE

Imagine the most mysterious and dangerous underground cavern ever yet discovered. Imagine that it is vast beyond easy comprehension. It stretches 10% longer than the Grand Canyon. Or, it is longer than the distance between Dallas and Houston. It is twice as wide as the Grand Canyon. Or, it is about the width of Dallas and Tarrant Counties, together, side by side.

The depth of the cavern, from floor to ceiling, is five times the depth of the deepest part of the ocean. The ceiling of the cavern is at a depth of ten to twelve miles, and the floor of the cavern is at a depth of 45 to 60 miles.

Above the main cavern, an upper, much smaller chamber stores the material from the lower cavern. The upper chamber is about 50 miles in diameter, and about 5 miles deep, or tall, or thick.

The top of the upper chamber is within 5 miles of the surface of the crust, where people live.

Wolves, bears, foxes, coyotes, eagles, otters, badgers, wolverines, elk, moose, and bison also all live there. The upper chamber is the huge magma dome for the world's most powerful and deadly super-volcano: Yellowstone.

Yellowstone is the world's largest and most active super-volcano. All of the pretty geysers and bubbling mud puddles are acting that way because something like the Earth's largest hotplate is just under ground a few miles, bringing everything in the frying pan to a simmer, just before it boils over in the world's largest explosion.

Yellowstone is on a cycle of about every 600,000 years, and the last explosive eruption was 640,000 years ago. The monster is overdue.

Yellowstone is unique among all volcanoes, including a couple of dozen other known super-volcanoes all over the world. Most of them are long extinct, and pose no modern danger. Most of them are located near the edge of a tectonic plate, where magma can break through the outer crust layers more easily. Yellowstone just burned its' way straight through the continental plate. It acts like a slow-motion monster laser, cutting and burning its' way up through hundreds of miles of solid rock, until it bores a hole out to the air, and explodes.

The main cavern has a gigantic hole in the floor of the cavern, under the eastern end, the same end where the upper chamber is located, and where Yellowstone Park sits precariously perched upon the eggshell thin roof of the world's largest super-volcano. How thick and solid is that roof? Well, Yellowstone has mountains, and cliffs, and all sorts of rugged landscape features, including several two mile tall solid rock mountains. The roof is several miles of "solid" rock, but when the magma down below stirs, it shakes the "solid" rock roof on top of it.

Imagine a gigantic lava lamp. Only, it really is lava! As it is super-heated way down in the core of the Earth, it rises in a hot stream, toward the surface, as far as it can go, overcoming gravity and breaking through, or burning through, solid rock all the way up. The upward moving stream is called a "magma plume", and can flow in the same spot for many millions, perhaps billions, of years. Whatever the mysterious structures at the core of the planet, something is happening there which makes molten rock so extraordinarily hot that it forces its' way up, even burning right through a continent.

Usually, the idea of the main cavern having a hole at one end in the floor would suggest the idea of a drain of some sort. The hole is about 100 miles in diameter. It is not a drain, but quite the opposite. It is a high-pressure feed tube for all the molten magma in the main cavern, and the upper chamber. Using seismographic waves, and very sophisticated computer programs, scientists have been able to "see" the main lava tube of the main cavern, extending down at least 400 miles, and certainly, it extends many times further down than that, straight down to the core. So far, just 400 miles, and that's as deep as we can "see". The scariest part is that the tube does not diminish as it goes deeper. Instead, it grows wider and wider, the deeper it goes.

The lava tube of a volcano is the restrictor on just how much lava the explosion can release. The greater the diameter of the lava tube, the more of an explosion happens when it blows. Most volcanoes have a diameter of less than a mile, but some of the super-volcanoes range from 8 miles in diameter, to Yellowstone, about 50 miles in diameter.

As far as we can tell, the main lava tube, the lower one, and the main cavern, the gigantic one, have never yet released their pressure directly, all the way to the surface. If such a truly Earth-shattering catastrophe did ever occur, it would likely terminate all flesh life upon Earth, by means of ultra-winter, and it would likely split the continent into fragments, and could damage the planetary structure and balance. The tilt of the axis could be changed, as could the rotation speed. That powerful a surface explosion could also radically alter the magnetic field of the Earth, leaving anything that did survive the blast exposed to solar radiation storms.

As scary as the prospect of a nuclear war may seem, it would likely leave several million or even billion survivors. If a major explosive eruption happens again anytime soon, and the volcano doing the exploding is Yellowstone, nearly everyone in North America would die within a few hours, or days, at most. A superheated storm of poisonous gas, called a pyroclastic flow, would spread out from the volcano at several hundred miles per hour. A column of ash and smoke would reach orbit, and cloak the whole Earth in soot and darkness. The initial shockwave from the first blast will race out long before the pyroclastic flow, with the air so compressed that it acts like a speeding steel wall, flattening everything for hundreds of miles in all directions. That initial shockwave will travel faster than the speed of sound, like battleship armor moving at around 1,000 miles per hour. As the cloud rises to space, it will be a classic mushroom cloud, but so huge that it will be seen from the entire continent, if the blast happens in daytime. The cloud will generate its' own weather patterns, and start many other storms as spin-offs. The flash of the explosion will be visible as far away as the nearest star, Alpha Centauri, but not until four years later.

The magnitude of the initial Earthquake from the blast will be unlike anything human minds have even known could happen. The entire North American continent will tremble and quiver, with mountains splitting in half, and entire mountain ranges being swallowed whole into the ground, and the whole ground rolling like ocean waves in a heavy storm, and rivers reversing in their flow, and lakes and all large bodies of water generating local tidal waves from the shock wave, and the effective end of the U.S. in this world will be upon us. In many ways, we might be considered the lucky ones.

The rest of the world will not escape, either. As the darkness over head thickens until almost no sunlight at all can enter the atmosphere, the temperatures will lower astonishingly. Within a week, a difference of more than

100 degrees would happen, and all of the world would freeze over. If the endless choking ash from the blast did not suffocate everyone else in the world, the subzero cold or starvation would finish them in a matter of days, not weeks. Better, some think, to go fast, in the initial blast.

All right, we know that nuclear war is no joke, but neither is Yellowstone. Yellowstone will not sign a non-aggression pact with us, either. There is no possibility of something like a "mutually assured destruction" concept as a deterrent, since Yellowstone only has one goal in mind: detonation. Destruction is not its' primary purpose. It exists to release unendurable high pressures down deep inside the core of the Earth, lest the very planet should perhaps split apart. Nonetheless, it does not care a tiny bit about the entire human race, or just how much it kills, or just how miserable those deaths might be.

Yellowstone is under orders from planet Earth to release pressure, at all costs.

Ground uplift, continual small Earthquakes, variations in the cycle times and intensities of the largest geysers, the rise of one end of Yellowstone Lake, the recent growth of a giant underwater plateau (like a huge growing cliff, with a flat top, which is about 100 feet tall, and a half mile long), and many other strange and unusual events occur routinely, there on top of the world's largest volcano. In 2003, a family of bison was found unexplainably dead, with no wounds, sickness, or poison apparent. The most likely killer was carbon dioxide, which kills just like that. The deadly, invisible gas came up from the ground, released from the magma below.

When sulphur dioxide is being released in great abundance by an active volcano, the upcoming eruption event will usually be low energy, like the lava flows on Hawaii. When carbon dioxide is being released in great abundance by a volcano, the upcoming eruption event will usually be highly explosive, like Mount St. Helen's.

When the magma is at great depth, the gasses are dissolved into the liquid rock, like the fizz in a soda pop. As the magma nears the surface, and the pressure lessens a bit, then some of the gasses escape, as when one opens a soda pop. The lower pressure lets the dissolved gas bubble out of the liquid. When the magma nears the surface, carbon dioxide rises up through the ground, killing bison.

There have been numerous documented cases where a magnitude 7.0 or greater Earthquake triggered an immediate volcanic eruption, as deep layers of rock were fractured or moved aside, allowing magma to vent. By the Richter scale, a magnitude 8.0 is ten times stronger than a magnitude 7.0. In August, 1959, Yellowstone experienced a 7.5 magnitude Earthquake. A 7.5

magnitude is five times stronger than a magnitude 7, which is the usual threshold trigger level for volcanic eruption activation. Of course, this depends upon many other factors, primarily, just how close to minimum pressure threshold has the magma been charged. It will erupt, no matter what, when it reaches its' maximum containable pressure, trigger or no trigger.

Taken all together, the signs, the activity levels, the activity types, especially a major Earthquake, in the last 55 years, ought to be a wake up call. Yellowstone is long overdue to blow, and it is ramping up right now to explode, like something the human brain cannot grasp. There is nothing we can do about it, except to recall that King Jesus Christ told us that there would be Earthquakes in various places, war, pestilence, famine, fire and brimstone (just what a volcano produces), and a third of the people in the world will die, and the Sun and the moon will not give forth their light, and then He will return, to save anyone left here who still believes in Him, and obeys Him.

Does anyone else notice that the very things which we were told would be present upon Earth, in the very last days, at the very bitter end of the "Great Tribulation", are precisely the things which would be present immediately after an explosive eruption of Yellowstone? Could such a parallel be more than a coincidence?

There is a great deal of reassurance in those thoughts, however. Since no one would survive very long anyway, if Yellowstone goes, it cannot possibly happen more than about two weeks right before King Jesus Christ returns, openly, in Power. Otherwise, all that He would find here would be frozen Christians, turned to ice, along with everything else. Nothing could live through total darkness, deep layers of choking ash, air too smoky and ash-filled to breathe, and minus 120 degree temperatures, as well.

"If those days had not been shortened, no flesh would be spared, but for the elect's sake those days were shortened." Notice, it records those "days": not weeks, months, seasons, or years. No flesh could last more than a week or two, tops.

BLESS THE MAN
WHO BLESSED THE MOON

For many thousands of years, people of all lands had looked up at night, and had seen a strange and beautiful little sister planet to Earth. At a distance of a quarter of a million miles, it was never possible to know for certain precisely what the surface of the moon could actually be like, or what unknown and undreamed mysteries would someday be discovered there. Only one or two facts never changed: the moon was still there, unchanged, and the human race could never figure out a way to actually stand there, and walk upon the surface of another world. (By latest scientific classifications, the moon is defined as a "dwarf planet", and is similar in size and overall general appearance to the Kuiper Belt Objects, which include dwarf planets. The Kuiper Belt is out beyond the main planets, but closer in than the Oort Cloud.)

The moon seems like the other inner planets, which are the solid rocky cores remaining from the original inner gas giants, which were shredded apart when the Sun exploded into life. Most likely origin for the moon is initially a part of rocky Mars, which still had oceans, until a major impact shattered Mars into its' present large remnant, and our own moon. The trauma was most likely a part of the initial ignition of the Sun, except that something very massive slammed into Mars, back when the moon was still part of it. One distinct possibility is another planetary core, even closer in than Mercury, which split Mars, and splintered into the multitude of rocky planet remnants known as the Asteroid Belt. The moon was apparently sheared off into a wide astray orbit, until it was snared by the gravitational field of Earth, and fell into stable orbit around its' new parent planet, as a happy adoptee.

So, things remained about the same, and "men upon the moon" was absolutely impossible, until July 20th, 1969. That day, instead of allowing a computer (less sophisticated than a modern digital watch or cell phone) to mistakenly wreck the first human expedition to the surface of another planet, a man named Armstrong judged that the lunar module was tracking a little long, in its' landing approach, and was likely to miss the best pre-chosen landing zone. He switched off the auto-pilot, and grabbed the joystick, and manually flew the L.E.M. safely down to a soft contact with the Sea of Tranquility.

As chief pilot, and Mission Commander, it was appropriate that Neil Armstrong be the first human to set a boot upon the lunar surface. As soon as he had done so, thousands of years of millions of strange human dreams about us one day walking upon the moon finally came true.

It is also appropriate that we still remember and honor him for the great flying and landing job which he achieved that day, which was a very real, and a very dangerous thing to do. Without Neil Armstrong, there would likely be no moon landing, or at least not one without a crash and tragedy. The U.S. might have given up, and Russia might have gotten a man there and back safely first, instead.

Now, imagine what would have happened, if once safely down upon the moon, the astronauts had climbed back into the L.E.M., and wanted to come home to Earth, but were stuck upon the moon, and died there?

That actually almost did happen. The single, with no backup, rocket motor for the return launch from the lunar surface was very simple, for dependability, in design and mechanism. A simple switch upon the control console fired the plain rocket, and off they went. Or, so it was supposed to go.

What happened was that when they were back onboard, with the hatches all sealed, and ready to launch, they hit the switch, and nothing happened. All that was heard was loud heartbeats, and ragged, nervous breathing.

When men are in space, they wear spacesuits, with heavy, insulated gloves. If they took off the gloves, their hands would freeze immediately. With gloves like that on their hands, they could not possibly rewire the circuit. If they were willing to sacrifice a hand to do the job, the hand would freeze solid before it could finish the repair. People say the phrase "worst case scenario", but, unless they are referring to something like that, I think those two astronauts win that contest.

While it is not known what prayer the two astronauts prayed next, it is reasonable to assume that they prayed one. Apparently, a third Traveler was along with them for the whole journey. He heard their desperate prayer, and said "Okay, I will!"

A split second later, the less famous man on the mission, Buzz Aldrin, almost certainly guided by the Lord Holy Spirit, grabbed a metal "astronaut-pen" in his heavy, too-thick-to-repair-anything glove, and shoved it with all of his strength into the place on the console where the broken switch had once been mounted.

MIRACLE!!! Instantly, the rocket motor fired, and two very thankful astronauts tried not to turn cartwheels for joy, as they watched the moon fall away below them on their safe way back to rejoin the main craft for the journey back to Earth!

So, if you wish to summarize the principle points, the men that landed mankind safely upon the moon for the first time, were King Jesus Christ, and

Neil Armstrong. But, the men that returned mankind safely from the moon the first time were King Jesus Christ, and Buzz Aldrin. It would never have worked at all, without all three of them doing their own parts right.

There is another wonderful thing which Buzz Aldrin did, while they were upon the surface of the moon, and, it could be one of the reasons why King Jesus Christ was so ready and willing to answer "Yes!" so immediately, in time of need.

Buzz Aldrin observed the Holy Communion of our good Lord, King Jesus Christ, once they had landed, before they left the capsule. Once he had, in full faith, and humble obedience, blessed the good Lord, the men, the mission, and the entire moon, the success of the effort was insured.

There was no way that the good Lord was going to allow brave men of true courage, and humble, obedient faith, to be defeated by the devil, or by a broken switch. The Earth was cursed, because of sin, back in the days of the Garden of Eden, and we did lose astronauts to fatal accidents upon Earth. But the moon has been blessed, by two believing, obedient Christians, and we never lost an astronaut there.

So, wherever we go exploring out in the Solar System, one of the primary training exercises which should be mandatory for all outward bound astronauts should be prayer and blessing. They should bless the good Lord, they should bless all of the people involved in the mission, and they should always bless the planet upon which they are seeking to land.

Now of course, some folks are likely to scream some nonsense about separating church and state. Let 'em scream! I think we would still rather have the best possible blessing and co-operation from our good Lord, so we can bring all those brave astronauts home safely.

If those jerks keep screaming about such ridiculous nonsense, maybe we can arrange a trip to Mars for them? (Then we can see if they want to keep prayer out of the space ship, when it's their skin on the line!)

FOUR SHOTS LEFT

The archeologist was back at work in Israel. The visit back to see his family in the U.S. had been wonderful, but the main focus of his thoughts was searching all over ancient Israel, hunting for forgotten or yet undiscovered relics, ruins, and artifacts. He had already found quite a few, and now was highly regarded as one of the best research archeologists in the whole world.

He was driving in his jeep, along with his wolf, in the region that had been approximately the western border of Israel, in the days of King Saul. He was looking for ruins or relics from the Philistine army, at the time of their strongest push against Israel, to try to overrun and conquer the smaller Hebrew army. (The Hebrews were still reconstructing their army, and they did not have enough men yet, or enough swords, either, even for the men that they did have.)

He came over a small ridge top, and stopped to look down into the little valley that was formed by the surrounding hills and ridges. The main sides of the valley ran parallel to each other, and enclosed a large flat bottom expanse of a possible battlefield, about a mile across, from side to side. The valley ran for almost ten miles, until terrain flattened out further down to the southern end, and there the valley sort of blended in to the rest of the small hills around there. After a few moments of examination, he picked a reasonable path down the slope of the ridge, so he could drive the little jeep all the way down to the floor of the valley, which he did. As he shut off the jeep, on top of a small rise in the center of the valley, he hopped out, and so did his wolf, which began sniffing everything around them in ever widening circles. The archeologist let him wander, knowing that the wolf would not choose to go very far from him.

As he was scanning the ridges, with his binoculars, he searched for any sign that a wooden structure might have once stood along the ridge tops, like maybe a general's headquarters, or something. Suddenly, he noticed that his wolf was sniffing a spot only a few yards away, near the very center of the little hill where they had parked. He was scratching a bit at the dirt, too. The man instantly went over to have a look. The long nose of the wolf could find many hidden things, some even left outdoors in the weather for centuries.

When he got there, the wolf looked up, wagged his bushy tail, and watched patiently, while the man began to closely examine the dirt where the wolf had been scratching. A minute later, he saw something like a small fragment of nearly disintegrated leather, which looked like the world's oldest little piece of goatskin.

His curiosity had to be controlled, as he snapped several photos, and then stopped to feed his wolf, so that the hunter would wait contentedly, while the examination continued.

Next, he put on purple nitrile gloves, to avoid being hurled instantly into some strange dream/vision, which had been a fairly common event for the last two years. When he touched something of historical significance, he was usually transported to the setting where the relic had played out its' own important part in the history of humanity.

He cleared away more dirt, snapping photos all the way. Finally, he had the little scrap of leather cleared enough to carefully lift it out of the remaining dirt. As he brushed away the last little traces of dust, and slowly lifted up one corner of the scrap, he suddenly had to fight to calm his racing heart, and to keep his breathing slow and even.

There, right in the dirt, were four small, almost perfectly round stones. They were each about an inch in diameter, and likely had the spherical shape because of being several million years in the bottom of a creek, or river, where water constantly rushed over them, and rolled them around, until they were like small stone cannon balls. Apparently, they had been contained in the leather, which was most likely a shepherd's pouch to carry them. In the ancient world, arrows were like rifles, but slings were like pistols. For many, many centuries men had carried bows, arrows, swords, and slings, along with a few round stones to hurl from the sling. This must have been a man's sling-stone pouch. (The modern equivalent would be an ammo belt.)

After a few minutes, and a lot of photos, his hands had stopped shaking, so he put down the camera, and reached out to carefully lift one of the stones. As his gloved fingers touched it, his consciousness was suddenly flooded with a powerful vision, and he heard a blast from a shofar, and the answering shouts, in ancient Hebrew, from thousands of Hebrew soldiers. He thought he heard a deep-voiced, good-natured chuckle in his mind, and then he distinctly heard the good Lord say "Listen! If I want to give you a vision, a pair of little purple gloves is not going to stop Me!"

As he blinked his eyes, in the sudden harsh, raw, mid-day sunlight, he squinted toward where he heard the blast from the shofar, and he saw an entire army of Hebrews along the top ridge of one of the mountains at the eastern side of the valley.

He heard a shout in the distance behind him, and turned to see an entire army of Philistines along the top ridge of an opposing mountain at the western side of the valley, and stomping out toward him came something ugly and huge. There were two figures, one much, much larger than the other, like a child following an adult, except that the small one had a full beard, and was actually a six foot tall soldier, struggling to keep up, and keep his balance, while carrying a bronze shield which was longer than he was tall. The shield weighed about 80 pounds.

The larger figure in front was about ten feet tall, and very athletic and muscular. He moved like a towering war-machine, lumbering along, leaning forward, head lowered and huge glaring black eyes fixed on something or someone over on the Hebrew side. The ground shook with every one of his 500-pound steps. A Kodiak bear in his full fighting rage might not have been intimidated by that thing, but nothing much smaller would have dared face it.

The archeologist turned back to look toward the Hebrews, to see what the monster was tracking. He saw a very athletic-looking teenager, not yet six feet tall, maybe about 19 years old, racing toward the monster, shouting praises to Almighty God, and screaming dire threats at the monster, in ancient Hebrew! The youth appeared to be alone in his charge, but, since the archeologist was in a vision, he could also see things that normal sight could not. Inside the youth, and overlapping him, was the living green flame of the Holy Spirit of the Living God! The Face of God matched perfectly with the face of David, and they both simultaneously roared out a war cry that was much like the roar of an angry lion, about to kill a trespasser. The roar was so powerful, that it immediately knocked down the shield-bearer, and he just stayed down on the ground, curled up in a ball, quivering in terror for the rest of the time.

The roar even stunned the monster a bit, and his headlong crushing charge weakly stumbled to an unsteady halt, about 20 feet away from David, and the giant, returning to battle-ready, planted his feet, and lifted his spear (with a 14 foot long shaft about the size of a 4 by 4, and with a bronze spear tip that weighed over 60 pounds), ready to launch a fatal missile.

David slowed only a bit, just enough to smooth out his stride, and then, just 15 feet away, David released the first of the little round stones, straight at Goliath's ugly face!

Nolan Ryan would have been very proud of that "pitch" and the rock bullet smacked Goliath in the center of his forehead. When the giant saw it coming, he tried vainly to jerk his heavy head back out of the line of fire. If he had not moved a bit, the rock might have bounced off of his bronze helmet.

Instead, the rock smashed into, and sank out of sight inside the skull of Goliath. Before it stopped, it just performed a frontal lobotomy, battle-field style. Goliath's eyes rolled back in his dying head, and he fell backwards, making the ground tremble when he hit. His useless but enormous arms and legs twitched and jerked a few times, as the nervous system began to die.

David and the green Holy Spirit leaped over to the sword of the monster, worked it out of the sheath, and then, raising the 40-pound sword high over his head with both hands, and shouting praise to Holy God, David slammed the sword down into and all the way through the throat of Goliath, in one mighty stroke. Blood splattered everywhere, and the head and helmet rolled away a bit. The sword had also cut through the chin strap, and David used the tip of the sword to pry out the head from the helmet. He then grabbed the head by the long hair, and lifted it up high, so his brothers and all of the rest of Israel could see the evidence of final victory!

A tremendous roar of victory rang out from the Hebrew army, and David's brothers all led the charge down the mountainside to join him, all the way shouting "Praise God! That's my little brother! Praise God! That's my little brother! David, David!" (None of them thought about it at the time, but David was also the 11th son, just like Joseph had been the 11th son. Each of the 11th sons proved to be deliverers, and saviors for Israel, and both started out as despised and disrespected by their own brothers. All of the brothers later changed their minds and their hearts, once God showed them just how very special and unique their own little brothers really were.)

As they ran with all of their hearts on fire, the entire Hebrew army swept across the valley, lifting David and the head upon their shoulders, and shouting honor and praise unto God and David. After a few minutes, when the shouting had died down a bit, David had them put him down, and his brothers apologized for doubting him, and went on and on about how spectacular a warrior he had proven to be! David took it humbly, saying that it was God that had won the battle, which was the truth.

A few minutes later, David turned, looked toward the Philistine army, and said, to all the Hebrew army there with him, "Well, it looks like we still have some more work cut out for us today. If we don't finish it now, they will just try it again in a few years."

David looked around at the men with him, and saw Jonathon, King Saul's son, who had rushed down the mountain along with the rest. David held the head out to him, and said, "Please do me the honor of staying here, and guard the head and all of Goliath's armor and weapons, since this day they are mine, but are too heavy for me to use in battle. I will go with our soldiers, and we will kill all of the Philistines today, but you, the king's son, please stay here with a few men, and protect my spoils."

Jonathon instantly respected and admired David, and loved him equal to his own brothers. He agreed, and David and all the rest of the Hebrew army began to march, not run, but march, implacably, toward the Philistines. The Philistines were not feeling near as brave about now, but their generals said they would slowly torture to death anyone that ran away. A few hours later, those same generals were running for their own lives, throwing away even their swords, to try to run faster. David, and the Hebrew army, and the Holy Spirit pursued, overtook, and absolutely exterminated the enemy. After that, Israel had plenty enough swords and shields and helmets, even if they had once belonged to the Philistines. (The Philistines, like all Greeks, at least understood enough about making weapons, and the skills of blacksmithing, and basic metallurgy, and they made strong, tough weapons and armor. Many times in the years to come, those same captured weapons would shed the blood of the enemies of Israel.)

The archeologist suddenly was back in the cool morning of the present year, and looked down at the rock in his hand. As he mused about the vision, he wondered why David had taken five stones, instead of just one. Again, he heard a deep-voiced chuckle in his head, and the same wonderful, smooth, rich voice of the Lord spoke and said, in his mind, "That was in case he had to kill the shield-bearer, too, or if he needed a few more shots to escape back to the Hebrew side. He did not know if his own people would rush out to meet him, or if the Philistines would try to chase him, instead. That was just David's way of being sure he could finish the job, once started. I knew that he would not need the other four stones, but I let him gather them, so I then had him drop the shepherd's pouch here, for you to find, today!"

THE MYSTERY OF ELEVEN

Almighty God does things in echoing patterns. The things in Heaven are reflected in things in Earth. The Ark of the Covenant was known to represent the mighty Cherubs, hovering at each end of the Mercy Seat. When our good Lord was Resurrected, two of the real mighty Cherubs were seen standing, one at the head, and the other at the feet, of where the Lord Jesus had slept, in death.

In fact, the Holy Word of God reveals that all of the Divinely prescribed features, and dimensions, and functions of the Holy Temple of God in Jerusalem are reflections of precise things arranged in like manner, in the Holy Presence of Almighty God. These patterns were even first instituted in the Tabernacle in the Wilderness, and later brought to full bloom in Jerusalem, under King Solomon.

God also does such repeating patterns in numbers, and their special Heavenly symbolism. We know that three means the Trinity, seven means perfection, or completion, six means mankind, forty means the time of purification, such as forty days and nights of rain, or forty days and nights of being tempted and tested in the wilderness, alone, or forty years of wandering around in circles in the desert. Even the forty days in which the Hebrew spies were surveying the Holy Land was a time of cleansing, and purification, since all but two of the spies were found to have "dirty" faith, and they were disqualified, as was the rest of Israel, except for the two faithful spy-witnesses, Joshua, and Caleb.

(Interesting to note is that both King David and King Solomon each reigned about forty years, the same as the time Israel spent being trained and disciplined by God, and also being made ready for war.)

One of the most mysterious (and rarest) of all number patterns applied by our good Lord is the pattern of eleven. It seems to have started with Noah, the 11th from Adam. He was rejected by his own contemporaries, as he preached the truth, and built the Ark. Nonetheless, eventually, God proved Noah correct, and saved the world through Noah, too, and also destroyed all of Noah's enemies.

Another 11th level activation is noted in the life of Joseph, the 11th son of Israel. He also was rejected by his contemporaries, which were his own brothers, but years later, God proved Joseph correct, and saved the world, and Israel, through Joseph, and did not this time destroy Joseph's former enemies, which were his own brothers, but instead, managed to win them over to love, respect, and, yes, dwell in terror of

Joseph for the rest of their lucky-to-be-alive days.

One of the most often missed 11th level activations is David, who was the 11th son of Jesse. His ten older brothers were passed over for the anointing as the next King of Israel, and they resented him for it. They belittled and derided him, until the day that they watched him decapitate Goliath, and then they adored him forever after that. They also dwelt the rest of their lives in awe (and in mortal terror of crossing their little brother).

In modern times, theoretical physicists and mathematicians currently seem to be of the opinion that there are actually 11 dimensions. They claim that the math demands it. They say that the reason we do not perceive the other dimensions directly is that they are coiled up sub-atomically small inside everything else. Perhaps that is so.

A fascinating modern era correspondence to the "Principle of 11" (if you wish) is found in the U.S. space program. It was not until Apollo 11 that humans first successfully made it all the way to the moon, landed, and safely returned home to Earth!

One time King Jesus Christ told a parable about workers hired at various times of the day, by the same landowner, to go to work in the field that day for him. Some were hired early, some were hired at midday, and some were hired at mid-afternoon. The landowner went back at the 11th hour, and found still more workers to hire, and also hired them. The amazing surprise was that after the day's work, the generous landowner gave every man a whole day's wage. He faithfully kept his word to all of them, and even was expansive in his rewards, so that each man had enough to feed his family that night. (The rich, generous landowner did not want any of the children to go hungry.)

We should all perhaps remember that now, in these last days, we are in the real 11th hour. If the good Lord chooses to use some rather unorthodox folks to preach the Gospel, what is that to you? You follow Him!

We need the 11th hour workers, too. There is way too much witness and testimony and prayer yet to be given by the Children of Light, before our King returns! We need more preachers!

One more noteworthy occurrence of the "eleven" pattern is manifested in the eleven faithful Apostles. They also were rejected by their contemporaries, and ridiculed, and even murdered. Nonetheless, God saved the whole Earth, and Israel, through them, and then He converted their enemies to also be Christians, proved the Apostles correct, and took them Home to be with Himself, and eternal great glory. He also made all of us modern Christians to respect all of the eleven Apostles, and fear them, and their mighty words, so much that we base our lives upon their written testimony of our good Lord. Life, and death, and Eternity were entrusted unto those mighty, noble warrior-Apostles, and the future of the entire human race was set adrift, like eleven "messages-in-bottles", against all odds, long shots, unlikely to ever succeed.

Nevertheless, as God lives, His Word shall not return to Him void, but wherever He sends it, it will achieve His purpose, and return to Him, "mission accomplished".

King Jesus Christ is the Word of God, and He achieved the purpose of the Father, and then did return unto Him, "mission accomplished"! (He did it through a pattern of eleven, this time, too.)

BREAKING THE FANGS OF THE SERPENT

When the enemy first struck against Eve, it attacked her when she was alone, without Adam there to defend her. It is unclear where he was, but up until then, there had never been any evil to fight. How could he ever have guessed that she might need him there, since she had never needed him to defend her before that?

The weapons of choice of the enemy are always lies. The purpose of the enemy is always to steal, kill, and destroy. The enemy's lies against Eve were intended to steal her peace, kill her joy, and destroy her love.

Adam and Eve were living in Heaven upon Earth, quite literally. When a man is able to walk peacefully, without fear, and talk conversationally, alone with Almighty God, and roam the entire Earth forever, unrestrained, and unhurt, not even needing sandals, or a jacket, and then, to top it all off, Almighty God creates and gives to him the true woman of his dreams, how could anything other than Heaven upon Earth be the accurate description?

The three first listed foundational attributes of Heaven are love, joy, and peace. The enemy stole Eve's peace by a lie that caused her to feel insecurity. It made her to doubt whether or not she could fully trust God's Word, or, by extension, God.

Next, the enemy called God a liar, and then lied and said that Eve could actually become "like God" if she would just sneak a little bite of that fruit. Eve, just like Adam, had been created perfectly, fully already "like God", made in perfect image of Him, just like Adam. She did not have to become "like God", since she already was like God! This particular line of lies was aimed at killing Eve's joy, by making her think that she was not all that she was supposed to be. The lies were designed to cause inferiority.

The twin-fanged attack worked like a double-barrel shotgun. Eve was knocked back off balance, deeply wounded, feeling betrayed by God, and desperate to feel once more like she was up to standards, and therefore, accepted as "good enough". The agony in her broken heart destroyed her love for God, and His Word, and for Adam, and his companionship, and she wanted more to be "like God" than like Adam, any longer. She thought that the only way to stop the pain was to take a little bite of the fruit. (It was not a painkiller, but poison, even though the devil had lied, and had said it was good, and not evil, to eat the fruit.)

At the first bite, the enemy had successfully stolen Eve's peace, killed her joy, and destroyed her love. From that point on, she was living cut off from

God, and from Adam, and began the remainder of her life living in the first true version of "hell upon Earth". There was never a lonelier human, until King Jesus Christ hung upon our Cross.

Her love had been replaced with hatred, and selfishness, and a heartless disregard for the destruction she might cause to anyone else's life or happiness. Once she was damned, she no longer gave a damn.

She panicked, and thoughtlessly, selfishly, dragged Adam into hell with her, also by lies, proving herself to be the first willing slave of evil. Adam learned quickly, and pulled the same stunt the next morning, starting out the day by hiding from Almighty God, and when confronted, blaming the whole thing upon his woman. Instead of delighting to see God first thing in the morning, now they were afraid to be near Him. Once their perfect love for God had been destroyed, they dwelt in fear, from then on. It still is happening today, except where the Presence of the Holy Spirit drives out the evil, and restores the re-born heart.

King Jesus Christ said that He had taken back the keys of "hell" and "death". We can rest well tonight, knowing that He does not lie, and He is never mistaken. Is it possible that this is perhaps His Way of naming insecurity and inferiority? A closer look may be in order.

Insecurity is pretty much the opposite of peace. In Heaven, there is peace. In hell, or upon Earth, if controlled by evil, there is insecurity. People have long said that war is hell. War certainly is the classic cause of insecurity, in the ultimate extremes.

What about inferiority? We know that inferiority makes people take all sorts of unwise, often deadly risks. It can make people do dangerous stunts, have plastic surgery, marry the wrong person, buy something expensive which they do not need, or really want, and so forth. It can make people choose a career in show business, or politics, or law enforcement, or the military, or even crime. It can affect the choices of fashion, location, education, occupation, affiliation, and even nation. (If folks south of the Rio Grande felt less inferiority, from being right next door to the world's richest country, would they really want to try to move in down the block? Not likely, if Mexico were richer! Instead, people from the north would be moving down there.)

Inferiority can make a person do things which seem okay at the start, but which eventually can lead them to death. A classic example would be teenagers racing cars for thrills and bragging rights. All too frequently, the only thing to "brag" about is how horrible a wreck it was, and how sad all of the family and the friends of the young racers are now.

The Word of God declares that "There is a way which seems right unto a man, but the end thereof is death." Does that mean that inferiority is the direct cause of death? It may be possible, given its' close interlinking action with insecurity. Insecurity starts the dominoes falling, then, inferiority, the next domino, falls, and then temptation, to make an unwise decision, followed by the "entering into temptation", or committing a willful sin, which leads to death. "Every man is tempted when he drawn away by his own lust, and lust, when it is finished, brings forth sin, and sin, when it is finished, brings forth death." The lust might be for recognition, fame, riches, power, acceptance, or whatever seems to be the magic pass-key for the person being tempted. Temptation is always tailor-made for the individual. It fits like an Iron Maiden, or a tight noose.

Notice that the devil launched its' rebellious attack against Almighty God, the Father, directly, by assaulting God's daughter, Eve. The monster knew that a deadly wound dealt unto Eve would destroy Adam, and very deeply grieve God the Father.

At the time of the attack, God had not spoken the prophesied future, yet, about how the Seed of the woman would destroy the serpent. Therefore, it is unlikely that the devil knew that it was attacking the future line of the Son of God, since it is unlikely that it knew that the Son of God would ever be sent forth, into the world, to be born as a human being.

Also, it appears to be a valid hypothesis that the devil cannot ever directly attack the Holy Spirit, except by means of the unforgivable blasphemy, which is yet another lie. (It remains a spiritual perversion, and an abomination, and the good Lord will not dismiss it.)

The worm wanted Adam and Eve to become its' slaves, and to be thrown into the Lake of Fire to die a second death, along with its' own miserable tail, since it knew, suddenly, at the very moment that it first tempted Eve, that God would see, and hear, and know, and even had known before the world began! All that the out-smarted worm had done was to play right into God's waiting Hands, and now, the trap had snapped shut upon it, and the worm would never escape the teeth of God's trap. The devil was not tricked or forced into evil, but instead, it freely chose to do it. God knew that ahead of time, and prepared King Jesus to come win back the Earth, and oh, yes, all of the would-be-saved human beings, and all of the good animals there, also.

King Jesus Christ did save all of those who will be saved. He did not miss or forget a single one. Nonetheless, He did not, and will not, save a single evil spirit, at all. Anything, or anyone, that tries to hurt one of the little brothers or sisters of King Jesus Christ will have to make repayment, in full, not to the injured Christian, but to King Jesus upon His Throne, in Power. It would have gone much easier for the offender, if the restitution was demanded only by the Christian. King Jesus can, and will, make the evil ones stay alive for a longer, hotter time in the Lake of Fire, before He finally closes their account, and lets them finish their punishment unto death. (They will not get out, until they have paid the very last mite.)

We do not have to concern ourselves with that. The good Lord will balance all of the books, once He is done.

Meanwhile, how do we destroy the devil's attack, which is, in almost all cases, and against all humans, about the same in design, weaponry, tactics, strategy, and deadly effectiveness? What can stop such a vicious, sub-human cruelty?

It may perhaps help to be able to picture the whole thing in a concept something like this: the devil, or worm, is like a giant snake, or serpent. The two main piercing weapons, like a serpent's fangs, are insecurity, and inferiority. The sin is the evil bite, by the serpent, and is parallel to telling a lie. The lie causes the fangs, insecurity and inferiority, to puncture the heart of the victim, and, once insecurity and inferiority have penetrated into the heart of the victim, the venom, which is fear, is injected into the soul of the person.

"The fear of man brings a snare." When fear has taken root, it causes people to lust to be free of fear, since fear, whether consciously realized, or not, causes torment. The lust may be expressed as an attempt to seek validation through sexual contact, or money, or power, or manipulation, or any number of other weird behaviors, which all of us human types might perform, to feel better about ourselves. When people feel powerless to control their own futures, they strive to control everything around them as much as they can manage, by any possible desperate means. This is futility, in action.

Instead, an effective counter-attack strategy is to:

(1) Refuse to believe the devil's lie that there is anything, at all, about which to be insecure. Every single breath of our lives is a free gift from God. Until the last one comes, the devil cannot stop anyone from having God's free gift of breath, until God allows it.

The same thing is true of our heartbeats. If, as just proven, the devil, no matter how hard it tries, cannot stop God from blessing someone, in fact, anyone, in any way that He chooses, then what advantage to worry about anything at all, since God knows what we need, and meets those needs, better than we can, anyway. When you fall asleep at night, can you remember to keep your own heart beating all night? Can you remember to breathe, too? And can you do that all night, every night, all while totally oblivious to all external events in space and time?

(2) Refuse to accept the devil's false appraisal that you are less than what you should be. Yes, all of us, except for King Jesus, have indeed sinned, and have fallen short of the glory of God. Even so, we were made and built in His Image, and King Jesus has restored us to His Image, and the Holy Spirit is constantly reshaping us more and more into His Likeness, so we will each finally, truly resemble Him. As we mature, and grow in Christ, over time, by hearing, and obeying, His Words, we are being transformed, by the renewing of our minds. Until that full transformation is revealed, just try to remember that you are a re-born Child of the Father of Lights. We are literally "living Light", very much like our Heavenly Father, since we are re-born of Him.

(3) Constantly hit back with those two mighty counterpunches. "Take that, insecurity! I still have breath and heartbeat!", or, maybe it might be "Take that, inferiority! Not only was I made in the Divine Image of Almighty God, along with every other human, but I am re-born of the Holy Spirit, and a true Child of Light, and I am just precisely the Way that God designed and built me! If you have a problem with me, or try to call me inferior in any way, take it up with King Jesus Christ! I am Judged by Him, not you!"

Does this counterattack work? Absolutely! When you base your strategy and tactics upon the Word of God, which is Truth, and agree with His Word, instead of listening to the devil's lies, then, in time, whether it is a split second, or ten years later, you are going to receive a victory, because if you obey and honor God, then He will hear, and answer you. We will overcome, by the

Blood of the Lamb of God, and by the word of our testimony.

Just try to be tough, and stubbornly patient, and keep trusting Him. Sometimes He will answer you something like "Okay, I will, but not yet." Often, waiting to hold in your hands the answer, which you know is on the Way, is almost agony.

Still, it makes the deliverance even sweeter when it is finally given! Bless God Almighty, in the Name of King Jesus Christ!

THE LAST TIME I MET GWEN

It was good for us to have a chance to catch up again. A lot of time had passed, and a lot of changes had happened.

Of course, we had both aged, and our mighty young bodies had been modified, by time, and injury, and illness. Even so, we had each once been very strong and fit, and we had each grown up and continued in a life pattern that included much regular exercise. Over time, we had each recovered strength, again and again, and each one of us had fought back to regain mobility and durability. As a result of the grace of the good Lord, and our own persistent efforts, we each could still move around pretty well. Each of us still led an active life, and we each kept our own lives busy, with very full schedules.

It was Valentine's Day. For a week or two before that, I had been fighting off a sinus infection, no doubt a free gift from some thoughtless creature that sneezed or coughed all over me, while we were standing in line to pay for gas, or something.

I knew she was at work that day, so I did not want to call her cell phone, or disturb her while working. Instead, I called her house line, and left a voice message that, if she was not already scheduled for something else, I would be glad to speak with her after work, and to wish her a Happy Valentine's Day.

Although we had not been a couple for over 30 years, still, I had learned enough about how a gentleman treats a lady from my Dad, and also from my Mom, that I knew a woman, even if she is not currently your girlfriend, still needs some man, even if he's not her boyfriend any longer, to at least give her a card and a chocolate candy bar (Hershey' Special Dark, only, please!). The chocolate she will need immediately, since all women need chocolate constantly. (I think they are born with a chocolate deficiency.)

The card she will need over time, just so that, every once in a while, her eye can wander over to it, and she can smile a little smile, and recall that for that particular day, at least, some guy remembered enough, and cared enough about her, as a woman, to at least give her a card, and some chocolate.

One of my Mom's favorite and often repeated teaching expressions was "Give your flowers to the living!" That is a very wise strategy. How will they enjoy them, after they're gone away?

Even though I deliberately decided not to give her even a single flower, the concept was still applicable. (A card and some chocolate candy bars is one thing, but a gift of flowers on Valentine's Day is a different message, entirely.)

So, although I did not want to interrupt, if she had any other plans made, I also did not want her to feel forgotten, either, in case she did not have any other plans made. I figured if she wanted to talk, she could return the call. If not, she could erase it.

That turned out okay. She called me after work, and I drove the 70 mile journey, through heavy evening traffic congestion, all the way across DFW Airport, north Ft. Worth, and still about a 45 minute portion beyond that, to finally end up in the first stages of west Texas, out where the real country folks live. It was about 2030 by the time I finally made it past all of the construction and congestion around DFW Airport, and north Ft. Worth. As I arrived, I brought in a small box of the things I had carried out there to her. The card was a picture of Charlie Brown and Snoopy, lighting a rocket, and then standing back to watch it fly. When she opened the card, the rocket had exploded into a heart shape, and the simple message was "Happy Valentine's Day!"

I signed it "Joseph and Lobo". That is whom the cartoon was supposed to portray. She got it, and smiled.

As suspected, the chocolate was a huge hit. I had included several different sizes of the bars from gigantic, for home TV viewing, to pocket size, to keep available in her purse, when she needed a quick chocolate fix at work.

I had also included a new book for her, from Josh McDowell, which is "More Than A Carpenter" on one side, and then, when you flip it over, and it is also "The Life Of Jesus" on the other side. The second one is an interwoven Gospel, similar unto "The Life Of Christ, In Stereo". If you have ever read or seen either of those books, they are very helpful, to see how all the Gospel writers' accounts fit together quite well.

We sat and talked for a few minutes, and caught up on the personal news. She had escaped without major injury from a car wreck a couple of days earlier, when a dumb kid sideswiped her car. The car needed repairs, but, thankfully, she was only sore, not broken. I had a flood in my house to dry out, when a hose to the washing machine had ruptured, sometime in the middle of the night, and the thing had flooded the house for the next four hours, while I slept peacefully, at the other end of the place, never hearing the water run. (Oh, well, the good Lord did indeed inform us ahead of time that in this world, we will have tribulation!)

All the time I was there, I kept noticing a quiet little smile staying around the corners of her lips. I think she was pleasantly surprised, and very happy, to have someone remember to bring her a card, and some good chocolate. (Every woman needs something like that, and I think it sort of stuns them when we remember to do something nice for them.)

I told her the progress, which was current on the books, and let her know that I was intensely overworked right then, struggling to finish book seven. She understood, and was, I think, mainly thankful for the nice, thoughtful surprise. We only visited with each other for about a half hour, and then, since I knew she had to get up early to go to work, I took my leave, wishing her a pleasant night's rest, and a speedy continued recovery from the sore spots from her wreck.

As I headed back eastward, into the night, I realized I was not riding off into the sunset, but instead, I was riding off into the rising moon. I will explain further.

Gwen and I had had our time, a third of a century ago, and it was a very sweet time, indeed. She was the first girl I ever really wanted to marry, and have lots and lots of grandkids with. Sometimes things do not work out the way that you hope. When that happens, you have to make other plans.

Gwen made other plans, and I did, too. In each case, a third of a century's worth of other plans was what we planned, and lived out. Even with all of that, Almighty God had other plans, still, and He could easily wait a third of a century to manifest them. That is what He did.

It was a total blindside, and yet a wonderful surprise, when I came in, one day last summer, and there was a voice message from Gwen, after 32 years of silence. I immediately returned her call, and we talked for hours, and a week or so later, we met again, caught up, and visited with each other for a couple of hours here and there, about once a month or so, over the next six months.

We got to know each other as new friends, with some echoes from the past, but never became a couple again. We talked about a lot of things, and some of them had needed talking out for a third of a century. Back in the old days, we had hurt each other's feelings, a few times, and it was needed for us to talk it all out, and to make peace at last, so healing could begin, even way down deep inside.

We both prayed together about things, and forgave each other, and we now have no lingering resentment or bitterness left to weigh our hearts down. We only want what's best for each other, even if that's someone else, instead of us. Finally, our friendship, and our Christian love for each other, is beginning to bear mature fruit into our lives.

Nonetheless, we have grown in much different directions in our time apart. She has her own interests, and I have mine. The schedule she lives, with full time work, and extra studies after work, and on weekends, is quite intense, and my own schedule is so loaded full, with writing every single conscious minute, that it is extremely difficult for us even to spend any time together, at all. That's life, in our modern 21st Century age.

While one would hope, and pray, that we will always be in touch, and always on friendly terms, now that that gift has been returned unto us, only Almighty God knows the future. (I never even knew that I would ever talk to her again, before Heaven.)

I still remain, and will remain, thankful that I ever was privileged enough to meet her, know her, love her, and always have the memory of a very blessed time in my life with her. I am living under a different set of mission orders now, and must continue to record whatever dreams or revelations are given unto me. That command is paramount for me. My mission will be accomplished, before my extraction, or without it. The good Lord will get me home, one day, one Way, His Way.

For now, I have to dream, and I have to write. This command I have received. I will obey. One of the prices I must pay is total concentration upon this matter, and I do not have time for social activities any longer.

Gwen and I will still likely be in touch once in a while. Essentially, she has her own life to live, and I have mine. She has her own mission in life, and I have mine. Each of us should finish, and do it well, and on time.

The age of the end is upon us. We will see the rise of the "moon", as the symbol of the Islamic confederacy of nations against Israel, and the West. I am called into battle, and my weapon is my keyboard. It will record truth, even if it hurts some folks' feelings at times. I will try to be diplomatically gentle, but not "politically correct". There is nothing at all correct about politics!

So, as I drove off into the rising moon, I saw the vision and symbolism of it instantly, as soon as my tires touched the east bound highway. Heading into darkness, knowing troubled times are certainly coming, and sacrificially leaving behind any hope of a closer relationship or future involvement with Gwen, until Heaven, I willingly headed into the fight against lies and darkness. I still have not yet finished my total mission. By the grace of God, I will.

You see, I am not heading into the darkness alone. There is Someone with me. He is very big, and strong, and smart, and He sees in the darkness, too.

TWO SHARP EDGES

When King Jesus Christ ascended back to Heaven, He told us that all Power and Authority in Heaven and Earth was given unto Him. We know that King Jesus never lied, and He never was mistaken, even about seemingly minor things. We also have noticed that He is absolutely the Master of understatement. We can rest very confidently in the certain fact that the Holy Son of God indeed has ALL Power and Authority, in Heaven and Earth!

We know that God and His Word are "One". We know that the Word of God does not return to Him void. We know that the Word of God is sharper than any two-edged sword, piercing even to the dividing asunder of joint and marrow and soul and spirit, and is a discerner of the thoughts and intents of the heart.

We know that King Jesus Christ is the Living Word of God, born as a human, died as a human, and Resurrected as the Firstborn from the Dead, and He is alive for evermore!

Notice that He lists two primary attributes which are now granted by the Father exclusively unto King Jesus Christ, upon His Resurrection from the dead. He now has ALL Power and Authority. He has it ALL, not only in Heaven, but also upon Earth! (Think a moment about that.)

We also have been instructed by the Word of God that the things done in Earth by God are reflections of things done in Heaven, following Divinely-set patterns.

Another place where the sharp two-edged sword is portrayed is in the first part of Revelation. There the sword is described as proceeding forth from the mouth of King Jesus Christ, upon His triumphant Return. The Lord also said that He had come to set a sword in the earth, and He would set some folks on one side of the sword, and some on the other.

Certainly, these are interesting, important, and eternal issues, which are absolutely worthy of deep consideration. The question presents itself, however, "Just what does that have to do with 21st Century science, including astrophysics, new technologies, space exploration, world hunger, taxes, traffic, back pain, headaches, traffic, taxes, and yet more headaches?"

There does appear to be a connection. As science gropes in the dark to try to understand matters much too vast and complex for the puny human brain, even the best theoreticians and researchers often spend many years, if not centuries pushing stubbornly down a dead-end line of reasoning. Remember the whole "flat Earth" world view that plagued mankind for all of recorded history, until a radical

Portuguese sailor/fortune-hunter/con-man accidentally "discovered" the Western Hemisphere. (The Vikings had beaten him there by about 500 years.) Hah!

Another classic example is the so-called "unbreakable" atom. Hah!

There was a time when people thought they could turn lead into gold, using a so-called "science" known as alchemy. Hah!

Even the finest minds in science often overlook the very basic facts, once their focus becomes locked into a particular "box" of thinking. They repeat the same pathways of inquiry again and again. Sometimes, as in the case of Thomas Edison, that may be the only way to make a working light bulb.

That does not make it easier to see the forest for the trees. In the case of the grand structures of the Creation, we can observe only a very tiny fraction of the things which exist, given the limited range and focal clarity of our primitive telescopes. Hale was not used for the first time until 1949, and ever since Mt. Palomar went into operation, we first discovered things like quasars, super-vast voids in space, monster black holes at the center of every major galaxy, and so forth. Hubble helped us even more, as will the new arsenal of all sorts of telescopes and observing devices mankind now has pointed out to the most remote regions of the sky.

Looking in the other direction, we can only see just so far down into the microscopic, or even maybe just catch a fleeting glimpse of the sub-atomic. The eyes of mankind were only meant to see within certain limits, at least, in this lifetime. God still wants us to look, as far as we can, just so we can see that He really, truly is an unlimited God, an infinite Creator, and that He makes infinite things, or at least, things so huge, that it tests us to our very limits to even see little computer-generated graphs and charts, of the real, enormous mega-structures and micro-structures which our good Lord has designed, built, and kept running, just fine, without our help.

The Word tells us that Jesus is the perfect image of the Father, and that someone that has seen Jesus has seen the Father. We are told that God is love. Jesus showed Himself to be Living Love, like the Father, when He gave His life for ours. The Father showed us His love, through His Power and Authority, which He has granted in full unto King Jesus, and the fact is that He always had that Power and Authority, since He really always was God, in human flesh, but He did not use a trace of His Divine Power and Authority upon the Cross, or it would have been cheating. He just made it through by being the very toughest Man Who ever lived!

The first action ever done in making the Creation was when the Father said "Be LIGHT!" By the Power of the Word of God, light is still shining, and the darkness cannot put it out.

The next part of Creation is when the Father separates the light from the darkness, and the waters from the waters, and establishes the Firmament. In modern scientific terms, the Firmament would be called the Universe. The Word tells us that God said unto the waters, "Thus far shall you come, and no farther!" God set the appointed boundaries even of water, and He enforces it as He wishes.

God did create the water by His Power, but He does govern it by His Authority. All things which God created were made by His Power, but He governs those things which He has made by His Authority.

Jesus did things in like manner. He created new eyesight for blind people by His Power, and He cast out demons, and rebuked deadly fevers, and even death, by His Authority. Perhaps this is why He stressed those two features of all the things which were included in His inheritance, upon His Resurrection. The main operational gifts, to continue to bring forth the Kingdom of Heaven upon Earth, are Power to create, as He makes all things new, and Authority to govern, as He deals out perfect Justice and Judgment.

A sharp, two-edged sword works best when both edges are razor sharp, and the blade is wielded in battle by the strongest, toughest, and most deadly, undefeatable Warrior Who ever fought! The names of the edges are Power and Authority! The Warrior is King Jesus Christ!

That is a close diagram of how the good Lord manifests Himself, through His Power and Authority, in the spiritual realm, and how it often is revealed in visible, real space-time events, which are usually called miracles. A closer examination is now in order, of how this same structure is parallel to the Way that the good Lord has designed and built even the physical universe, using the structural components of energy, time, space, and matter.

(To continue our exploration of precisely how God's Power and Authority are mirrored and echoed all throughout all of Creation, even within all of the components of all of the physical parts, too, please continue into the next chapter. It is suggested that you may want to stop for a few minutes, and brew yourself a fresh cup of strong coffee, or perhaps tea, if you prefer. The next part is a bit complex, and yet, it becomes much simpler, once the newer viewpoints are discovered. Anyway, take a coffee break, and I'll meet you at the start of the next chapter in just a few minutes, after my own coffee break!)

THE MATTER OF GRAVITY

All right, the question arises as to how, precisely, does God's Power and Authority design, build, maintain, regulate, modify, and transform all of the physical Universe, as well as the spiritual, unseen (at least, by men) portions of Reality, which are still extremely real and solid. Are there fundamental components of Reality that can be closely correlated with Almighty God's Power and Authority?

All of the physical evidence of the "solid" Creation proves the absolute Power and Authority of God, but some researchers may yet discover a far more profound, integral involvement in even the foundational components of Creation. (The next few observations are radical, so please hold any automatic dismissal, until all of the facts are examined, and time for reflection by the reader has been fairly granted, with an open-minded, willing-to-explore-new-concepts approach. Everyone is encouraged to do their own personal research into these subjects, along with a lot of humble prayer and meditation about it. No two human minds understand every single thing precisely the same way. Examine, weigh, consider, and decide for yourself.)

God has revealed that He uses His Power to Create, and His Authority to govern. In the physical Universe, we can understand that God has used His Power, as expressed as Energy, to start the physical Universe, with the Big Bang, when He said "Be LIGHT!"

The light is still shining, and the darkness cannot put it out, ever. The things which have been crafted out of light, by Almighty God, include all of the mesons, bosons, quarks, electrons, protons, neutrons, atoms, elements, molecules, compounds, minerals, chemicals, dust particles, rocks, comets, moons, planets, stars, star systems, galaxies, clusters of galaxies, super-clusters of galaxies, and so on, whatever is a grander structure than super-clusters of galaxies. (Anything as big as that does not fit very easily into my skull.)

We now understand that the very fabric out of which everything which we see has been built is composed of some form of light. No one has yet figured out how God wrapped pure light up into little tight bundles called protons, neutrons, and electrons, but we do have all sorts of valid proof that such an astounding feat is precisely what He did!

All solid matter is built out of little bundles of light. Those little bundles of energy are atomic-sized, but they each contain a mountain's worth of bottled-up energy. To prove that point, a thing called the atomic bomb was designed, built, and deployed, twice, within a week, and that ended WWII. The amount of matter converted to energy was not much, since the detonation immediately separated and scattered all of the uranium, by vaporizing it in the first split seconds of the blast. The total amount of uranium needed to start the chain reaction blast was about the size of a softball, for each device. The weight of the material used in each case was less than 60 pounds. The amount of energy released was equal to thousands of tons of dynamite.

All types of energy are various forms of light, except for one. There is one form of energy, which has nothing at all to do with light, of any kind, at least, not any kind of light that we can see, or understand, unless one includes quasars, of which more will be said, later.

In the last few years, scientists have proven that black holes do indeed exist, and are not just some strange notion for sci-fi writers to use. They have even recently discovered that every galaxy has a central black hole, and, the more massive the black hole, in proportion to its' galaxy, the more likely that the galaxy will form a large spiral, just like our own Milky Way, and also our nearest monster neighbor galaxy, Andromeda. The lines of gravitational force extend out from the central black hole, and also incorporate the entire gravitational field of the combined, whole galaxy, and the spinning rotation of the central point focus of the gravity field moves the entire galaxy, spiral arms and all. The disk shape is produced by the rotational velocity of the whole galactic disk.

The mysterious, light-independent form of energy, with which we have a lot of familiarity, even upon Earth, is gravity. It does not proceed from light, or a black hole would cease to produce external gravity, once the light could no longer escape the event horizon. It does exhibit some similar characteristics as light, such as following the fall-off rate of the inverse square law, supposedly traveling in a straight line of travel, and being able to have some projected effect upon the surrounding environment, with the ability to produce change.

Gravity, matter, and mass are so much a part of our own bodies, our own ways of perception and understanding, our own ways of living, moving, and existing, that we often overlook some of the most obvious aspects. We become so busy using the tools, that we forget how they are actually designed and built, and so we sometimes miss getting the best results.

Matter cannot be created, or destroyed, at least, not by man. The closest we can come is either the nuclear bomb approach, or the super-conducting super-collider approach. For all mankind thinks that he knows about science, man cannot, and never will be able to actually make a single created new thing. All mankind can do is to try to find ways to modify or destroy what God has already made. We are limited to using what we have been given, and cannot make anything new on our own.

The various forms and fashions of God-Powered light are the raw material of which all is made, but gravity is the builder of those things. It is gravity which draws things together, where they form atoms, molecules, compounds, dust and gas clouds, planets, stars, star systems, galaxies, and so on. It is gravity which compresses all of the dust, until enough uranium and high-gravity-compressed hydrogen in the environment is dense enough, and pressurized enough, and then a valid critical mass of uranium is accumulated, and a detonation happens, down deep in the dust pile of a new, unlit star, and then BOOM! Ignition occurs. It ignites the hydrogen, into hydrogen fusion explosions. As soon as it goes into fusion, instead of fission, as long as there remains enough hydrogen to fuel the ongoing furnace, the star will keep burning, brightly.

It is gravity which keeps planets in orbit. It is gravity which keeps people from flying off into space from the surface of the Earth. It is gravity which keeps our atmosphere from also flying off into space from Earth. The oceans are kept here also by gravity.

Gravity is what causes a star to collapse, when the endothermic nuclear fusion of iron begins in the core of a dying star. As the heat is used up, as more and more iron is fused into existence, the pressure generated by that heat is also reduced, and the weight of the star material caves in the outer layers upon the core. The geometrically increasing internal heat and pressure then generated by the collapse of the entire star causes even heavier elements to form, just before the star goes supernova. The resulting explosion can usually be seen over most of the visible Universe. Those just-formed heavier elements are thrown far and wide, to condense into new stars and planets, and eventually, make a third-generation system, like our Sun, complete with heavier elements, like gold and such.

Gravity affects energy, time, space, and matter, but is not itself affected by any of those primary, foundational, component parts of the entire structure of the physical Universe! (Please stop a moment, and read that last sentence again, and think about it for a moment.)

Return to the lessons taught by the black hole. Matter cannot be destroyed, but it can indeed be converted into energy. (Even mankind can do that much, with fission and fusion.) The black hole strips matter of every sub-atomic structure, and converts 100% of the matter into raw plasma, which is kept locked inside the black hole, at least, as far as we can prove.

Within the event horizon, even speedy light (energy) is held captive. Time is constrained into near-eternity, from an observer's viewpoint within the field. Space is so severely curved, that it ends up wrapped impossibly tightly into an infinite inward spiral, down into nowhere.

The black hole proves that gravity is indeed the king of the Universe. Energy, time, space, and matter cannot resist it, or overpower it. Gravity is what builds galaxies and what destroys stars and super-clusters of galaxies, also. Gravity is what holds the entire structure of the entire Universe together, and causes it to act as a single unit, just like a whole spiral galaxy all rotates as one single unit, and a spinning super-cluster of galaxies all rotates as a single unit, and travels through the void, all together.

As accurately as we can tell at this point in history, there is something which has been called the "Great Attractor", and it is estimated to contain as much as 95% of all of the mass in the physical Universe. It is most likely the very first-ever-formed black hole, which has been steadily gobbling up planets, stars, solar systems, galaxies, and super-clusters of galaxies, ever since shortly after the Big Bang. (I doubt if it even burps any more, no matter how big a bite it swallows at once!)

It is like a gigantic, galaxy-eating alligator, that swallows everything whole, and digests it later, at its' leisure.

Whatever the Great Attractor ever turns out to actually be, it is the most massive single point in the known Universe, and, so, by definition of terms, it is the center of gravity for the whole Universe. Everything else with mass revolves around the Universal center of gravity, which is the Great Attractor. The inconceivably vast gravity field produced by that monster keeps the whole structure of the Universe acting just like our good Lord wants.

A few critical distinctions must be drawn between gravity, matter, and mass.

Also, a distinction must be illustrated, between gravity, and all other forms of energy, or light.

Matter is composed of the tiny little bundles of energy, or light, which form the things we understand as the building blocks of "solid matter". (These start at even more profound levels than proton, neutron, and electron, but that level will do for this discussion.) It does seem worth mention that most of the matter in the Universe is actually not "solid" at all, except in the sense that the protons, neutrons, and electrons are "solid matter". The stuff is mostly interstellar hydrogen, scattered all over the whole Universe, even in the great voids, where no stars ever formed. The amount of tightly bundled energy contained within the atomic components is staggering, as is illustrated by Einstein's famous formula. It was proven true, later, across the Pacific Ocean, to end the war.

Matter is the component of Creation which cannot exist without all of the other components. There must be energy, time, space, and gravity, too, for matter to ever form. Energy can exist without anything else, except a source. Time can exist without anything else, except that it must have energy to exist. To even begin to count time forward, there must be a beginning. That beginning requires energy.

Space cannot exist, without energy, to stretch it out, and time is also required, for the stretching to progress, and increase, forward and outward, from point zero. Space does not need matter to exist.

Matter can sort of be considered as "frozen" energy, although it is much more involved and complex, in the grisly details. Still, that is a good enough working concept for it.

Matter is that component of Creation which can, and is, directly affected by gravity, and was produced by gravity, which is the constructive agent which compresses all of those little bundles of light into bigger, and bigger, and ever more complex conglomerates, and atoms, elements, molecules, and galaxies.

The mathematics which our good Lord often uses is not square-logic, or linear, conventional math. He employs a lot of fractal math patterns, all over Creation. Fractal math exhibits certain characteristics, which include self-similarity, and infinite repetition. A close look at clouds, waves, trees, galaxies, and so forth proves this to be the case.

Matter possesses mass. Mass is that aspect of "solid matter" which responds to a gravitational field directly. Mass is what causes a thing to have weight, in gravity, and inertia, even in free-fall. (It takes a while to get it going, and then it takes a while to stop it.)

Matter is not precisely the same thing as mass. Again, at the event horizon of the black hole, all atomic parts of the matter are completely destroyed, or more accurately, stripped down into plasma, and are no longer "solid matter". Instead, the matter has now been entirely converted back into raw energy. Even though the matter exists no longer, the mass which it brought along with it, to the black hole, stays behind, wherever the "once-upon-a-time-was-matter-but-now-is-raw-plasma" stuff is sent, down inside the black hole.

The only thing not held captive by the gravity well of the black hole is gravity itself. Gravity is immune to itself. It goes on merrily about its' own business, no matter how much energy, time, space, or matter is present, or absent. It alone of all things created in the physical Universe will not be dominated or conquered by any other thing at all. Gravity is always positive. It only gets stronger. The effect of the field is intensified, the closer one gets to the focus. There is, despite what the unscientific sci-fi writers would tell you, no such thing as "anti-gravity". (By the Way, there is only one Universe. God did not need a second chance to get it right!)

Gravity can also affect energy, but not directly. A lot of misconception is around these days about that. Light cannot be bent by gravity, despite what is often said by even "scientists". Gravity curves the space, not the light. The light still continues traveling, always, in a straight line, and always will. If the space it is speeding through is curved into a closed loop, the light will follow the curve of the space in which it is moving. If it is inside the event horizon of a black hole, the light will go around and around in tight circles inside the black hole, but it will still be traveling in a straight line, all the time.

The newest understandings of time and space indicate that space and time are not really separate things, but are more like two sides of the same coin. Time and space are so very extremely interwoven that to change either one also changes the other one. The modern way to discuss this is using the term and concept known as "space/time". We can tell that gravity does indeed warp space/time, even within our own local little Solar System. That's what is causing the Earth to go around and around the Sun, over and over. The Earth is trying to fall in a straight line, but the warp of the space/time by the gravity well of the Sun is making the straight line come out as an orbit around the Sun. The moon is trying to fall in a straight line, too, but the warp of the space/time around the Earth, because of its' gravity well, is making the moon travel in Earth orbit. So, now it is becoming more apparent that what we always thought of as nice, stable, square, "3D space", and also, normal, "always-flows-forward-at-the-same-rate" time are not the ultra dependable, rock solid platforms which we used to think. Things change, depending upon a lot of variables.

Of course, no one human, except for King Jesus Christ, will ever fully understand all of the aspects of all of this. The point to remember is that He wanted to shape us out of dust, breathe the breath of Life into us, and charge us with the sparks of abstract thought, and reason, in our minds, in order that we might seek and try to know Him, as revealed by His mighty Word, and His mighty deeds.

A few of these mysteries still make me wonder a lot. For instance, since we know that light, or energy, has no mass, how can it be affected by gravity? The only logical answer to that is what we discussed earlier. The light still does travel in a straight line, even in a curved space. It just follows the curve of the space through which it travels.

That's fine for energy, but what about time and space? As near as we can tell, time does not weigh a single ounce, no matter how many billion years are put in the scale. The same observation can be made concerning space. No matter if we include a volume of space large enough to fit the entire Milky Way Galaxy within it, but if it is only empty space, without even hydrogen anywhere in it, it weighs absolutely nothing.

That's the part that stumps me. If space weighs nothing, and it does weigh nothing, how can gravity affect it? Time affects space by forming the matrix in which change can occur, to the space in question, in our case expansion, or warping, which appears as compression, from our outside viewpoint. So, energy expands things, but gravity contracts things. Energy stretches things out, but gravity shapes and limits the stretching out.

Another mystery is how time, which also weighs absolutely nothing, can be affected by gravity. The answer to that riddle must be that somehow, since we know that space/time is really two aspects of the same structural component, what affects one side of the component also is able to affect the other side of the component, since the two are tied together, forever. Maybe time, taken all by its' self alone, cannot be affected by extreme gravity, but space can, and so it modifies time, along with space.

We should look deeper into these mysteries. The Word of God declares that it is the glory of God to conceal a thing, but it is the honor of kings to search things out. The Word also decrees that He has made us priests and kings, for His Name's sake. Also, we are supposed to study to show ourselves as workmen approved unto God. "Study", He said. We had better study, if we want to obey Him.

Now if, in fact, this examination of energy, time, space, matter, mass, gravity, and the grand structure of the

Universe has not tied your mind into a hopeless Gordian knot of headache, and confusion, then congratulations! (Your brain is running cooler than mine, at the moment.) There still remain a couple of strange aspects to all of this which should be mentioned, before closing.

Please consider: we know that the matter is not the source of gravity. When the matter is destroyed, into the black hole, the mass, and its' gravity, stay behind, intact, just more concentrated. That's not the only puzzle here. The mass itself can not be the source of the gravity, either, since the mass did not exist, before the matter was created, by the condensation, compression, fusion, and other matter-creating processes, all of which are done by taking light, in some form or other, and shaping and compressing it into matter, using gravity, in the only form in which gravity ever appears. Gravity always saturates the entire Universe, and it is always attractive, never repulsive, and it only increases, and it has no upper limit. Gravity, when viewed with those characteristics in mind, interestingly resembles both Almighty God's Authority, and also Almighty God's almighty Love. God's Word also declares that God fills Heaven and Earth. Huh. Those are the same two places which He mentioned upon His Resurrection, in which He has all Power and Authority.

All right, since the gravity existed before the matter ever did, and the gravity continues even after the matter is destroyed, and gravity exists whether or not there is any time, space, or matter, therefore, it is not at all like any other type of force, or energy.

Energy requires a source, as when a star shines light into the night sky. The light comes from a specific source, which is required for the light to shine. Time and space are brought forth, when the energy continues to operate, and thus causes changes over time, such as the expansion of the Universe, and the formation of matter, with the passage of time.

We know that our good Lord said "Be LIGHT!" Notice that He did not say "Be GRAVITY!" The light is still shining, just like He commanded it to do. Gravity is still operating, also, as though He also commanded it to do so. Is it possible that He did not have to command the gravity to come forth, as with the light, because the gravity already existed? The Hebrew Scripture talks about the "Chabad", the "weight" of the Presence of the Living God. God declares in His Word that He fills Heaven and Earth. So does gravity. Is the structure of the Universe so designed and built that even the gravity is the manifestation of both the Divine Authority, and also, the weight of the Presence of the Lord, in every cubic inch of Reality, seen and unseen? God does create by His Power, and God does govern by His Authority. He creates by light, and He shapes and rules by gravity.

The baffling mystery of where does the gravity come from may be easier to resolve, if we consider this, that perhaps it is woven into the structure of the whole universe, and is actually what we are trying to discover, as "The Universal Field". We know that the matter is not the source, and we know that light is not the source, and we know that the mass is not the source, either, since the mass did not exist, until the matter was created, but the mass can not be destroyed along with every other part of matter. Mass is something different, than matter, and than gravity. Mass is the aspect of matter which is affected by gravity, as indeed are also space, and through it, time, and energy, but it is the aspect of matter which cannot be destroyed, no matter how extreme the conditions. Mass, indeed, does exhibit another common trait, with gravity, in that both of them are only positive, and cumulative, and both also are without upper limits. Neither gravity nor mass are affected by energy, time, or space, except for the inverse-square fall-off rate for gravitational field strength. Gravity, manifested into the Universe through mass, alters energy, time, space, and matter. Gravity is king of the Universe, and mass is his general. What gravity wants, he gets, and he uses large masses to exert his presence intensely, here and there.

Gravity is also present in the sub-atomic, and even though it is the weakest of the four forces, at that level, what enables gravity to completely overpower, and demolish into insignificance, all of the other three forces is that gravity piles up, higher and deeper. It increases insanely, until it cancels the effects of all other things, including the strong nuclear, the weak nuclear, and the electromagnetic forces. By the time matter makes it into the black hole, it has forgotten that it ever was "solid matter". Gravity, like mass, cannot be overcome by anything else. Instead, gravity overcomes everything else.

The concept which just will not let my mind alone is this: perhaps gravity is powered from outside the Universe, which would fit, if it really is the physical manifestation of God's Presence, and Authority. Why else would it be everywhere, even out in the middle of nowhere, and totally saturate the whole thing? (Even though being in space is supposedly "weightless", the simple fact is that some tiny micro-gravity does still saturate the entire Universe, even if it is too weak for our bodies to feel it.) Somehow, the Universe and gravity are so woven together, it is impossible to separate them. Mass is not gravity, or the source or gravity, but it is more like a conductor of the gravity which is already there, in the fabric of the Universe. Mass forms a focal point for the gravity, like a grain of dust in the air forms a condensation nucleus for a raindrop to form. (In a sort of similar concept, space/time is not the source of light, but space/time is the conductor which transmits the light through it/them.) When matter is created, gravity is the agent which builds it out of little bundles of energy. The little bundles of energy may be changed into raw energy again, but the mass remains behind, as part of the permanent change made in the Universe by Almighty God, using gravity.

The Word declares that the gifts of God are permanent, and when God has created a piece of matter, He does not usually intend to destroy it. He made the Universe to last, but mankind messed it up. Wherever the location is in the Universe, the "weight" of God is there.

He does not always choose to reveal His Presence, until He is ready. The

Prophecy of King Jesus Christ unto John, named the "Revelation to John", not the "Revelation of John", can reveal more unto a curious student, of how God does not always reveal His Presence, until He is ready, according to His Own Wisdom.

It is good to probe into the deepest mysteries of God's Way. He built the whole thing to make it practically workable, but He designed and built us to be able to understand and appreciate the marvels of what He does. God always does things in a grand Way. Just wait until the next clear, mild spring or summer evening, and go out, away from other lights, and look up in wonder, at the stars.

Consider the works of His hands, and ask yourself, "What is man, that You art mindful of him?"

While you're at it, the things which we should remember are to thank the Lord, hear the Lord, and obey the Lord. That's precisely what He said to do. After all,

He built the Universe out of His Power and Authority. It's best not to argue with Him!

THE PLACE OF DARKNESS, AND THE HOUSE OF LIGHT

In the book of Job, God asks Job many intense questions about nature, and the structures of Creation. Among the items included, God asks Job if Job knows the place of darkness, of if Job can find the path to the house of light.

Approximately 5,000 years later, in our modern 21st Century, we can maybe begin to finally answer those mysterious questions. To the very best of our latest scientific knowledge, there is absolutely no place darker in the entire Universe, than a black hole. No light can escape it, since the light is trapped inside a closed-loop of space/time, and just races around and around in tail-chasing circles inside the event horizon. The question poses itself, how can that be anything other than the definition of "the place of darkness"?

What about "the house of light"? Of course, in purely spiritual terms, the House of Light is the Kingdom of Heaven. Even so, since the context of the dialogue between God and Job is about nature, and the physical Universe, we must seek another candidate for that title.

We know that once, in the very beginning, the entire Creation, including every tiny bit of our present Universe, was entirely pure light, during and after the Big Bang. As near as physicists can estimate (and I do mean estimate, which is what almost all of "scientific" data amounts to, is just estimations, approximations, educated guesses and erroneous calculations, which are later proven vastly wrong), the greatest sources of light and any other type of active emissions in our present Universe are things called "Quasars" and "Blazars", which are strange luminous objects way, way out far in the Universe. The amount of light and other types of radiation produced by those monsters is on an order of magnitude far in excess of anything we have ever observed, anywhere else in Creation.

These strange objects have only been known to exist, by humanity, since the early 1960's. Some of them may have total masses in excess of 20 billion, yes, billion, solar masses. The gigantic black hole at the center of the Milky Way only has a puny mass of about 5 million solar masses. Even ultra-huge Andromeda has a central black hole of only about 200 million solar masses. Galaxies in any sort of normal structure, or environment, will not ever grow as massive as the largest super-quasars. (The only known object more massive than some of those huge quasars is the Great Attractor, which is thought to contain at least 95% of all the mass in the Universe.) We are not yet certain why normal galaxies do not grow that huge, but the really large objects are those quasars, and all of them are found at extreme distances from Earth. They are the most distant objects which we can see, and also, the very brightest, by far.

Many of those remote quasars are not nearly as massive as the really big boys, but all of the quasars emit far more radiation than they ever should, given the masses which they are "estimated" to have. Some scientists think that they are just enormous black holes that are in "active" mode (that is, eating galaxies) at the moment. There is a great flaw with that theory. Although we have detected and observed the presence of many black holes in much closer proximity to Earth, and we have also detected many "active" galaxies, where the central black holes are currently feeding, and actively emitting, we have not observed anything nearby that emits as much radiation as millions of galaxies, yet only is as massive as a single galaxy! That is one of the hallmark traits of a quasar.

Quasars are the most distant objects which we can observe, and that makes them the most difficult to analyze. We can approximate their mass, their distance, and their luminosity, and we can define which frequencies of emissions are being produced, but that's about it. Over a million bright quasars have been found, and over 60 of them are the ultra-gigantic quasars, and over 50 of them are the gigantic blazars. (Quasars and blazars differ in levels of emission, frequencies of emissions, and luminosity. The quasars are the brightest, and biggest, and most distant, and are the first of all classes of exotic sky objects discovered by direct observation, back in the 1960's.) The very brightest of them, even though at distances of up to 12 billion light years, or nearly to the edge of observable space/time, can be seen on a clear night with amateur astronomy equipment, and appear as faint, fuzzy stars.

One thing must be understood by this set of facts: whatever the quasars are, they are not what we understand as anything remotely like a "normal" black hole. The energy emitted from a black hole does not come from within the black hole, since no light and no radiation can escape the infinitely deep gravity well. The radiation which is detected from a black hole is from the destruction of matter as it enters the accretion disk, and releases the atomic energy stored in the particles, but that energy is released from just outside the event horizon, or it could not escape the gravity. No black hole, however massive, exhibits the quasar-level output of energy emission, which is insanely and outrageously off the charts, for any object no more massive than many of the brightest quasars calculate to be. Something that weighs as much as a galaxy cannot possibly produce as much radiation as a galaxy that would weigh millions, or, in some cases, billions of times more than it does weigh. Normal space/time does not allow for that to occur. Something else strange and mysterious is happening.

Modern scientists may have failed to see the larger picture, which correctly fits all of the missing pieces of the puzzle together. Even though Einstein mathematically understood black holes, he did not believe in them. Schwarshield and his math had convinced Einstein that something like that was possible, but he did not think God would allow such a structure to exist. It just seemed way too strange. (One wonders if he would have voiced the same objection, if he had been the scientist who discovered their possibility, instead of another man. Einstein often seemed to be convinced that no one else but him could ever understand the true nature of things.)

One of the things which neither of them saw was that a central black hole is necessary to form any really large spiral galaxies. Otherwise, the total gravitational field is not intense enough to keep the entire galaxy disk all together, moving and acting as a single unit. Another feature which they missed, since they did not know, as we do, that the Universe is accelerating outward, ever faster, and has not slowed down one whit, ever since the Big Bang, is that there is a vast amount of creative energy still being applied to the developing structure of the Universe, even this day.

Maybe the Big Bang faded over time, but now, there are many littler bangs going on all over the outer fringes of the expanding Universe. These are the quasars.

Everyone that ever saw an episode of Stargate knows what a "wormhole" is supposed to be. Unfortunately, none of the things portrayed during that entire series could actually happen, since for any human flesh to go anywhere near a singularity would mean immediate death, not amazing transportation through a vast distance. The only thing left inside a black hole (or any type of gravitational singularity) is raw energy. (Plasma. Nothing else.) No human body could survive such an experience.

(From this point on, please understand that the concepts which I will attempt to describe and portray in some comprehensible manner are a bit deep, and entirely unheard-of, at least, as far as I am aware. I am merely trying to do the things which I was commanded, in a powerful dream. I must try to accurately transcribe the concepts and visions placed in my strange dreams. If you do not think that it is the good Lord which sent me these dreams, please pray that He will stop them, or correct them, so that I can precisely communicate the concepts and pictures which I was shown, and write the truth.)

Let's consider the case of a crack in the crust of the Earth. It may only be a small, insignificant little fault, not even much of a serious fracture at all. Then, one fateful day, a surge of pressure from down deep in the core of the Earth heaves upward against that little flaw. Ultra-hot magma drives upward, trying to split open the planet. Suddenly, the unimaginable force from below widens the crack a tiny bit, and then with groaning and shuddering, the whole thing sort of gives up the fight, as whole underground mountains move sluggishly out of the way of the boiling liquid rock.

With a few last-second warning Earthquakes, the landscape explodes, and a blast of steel-solid, super-compressed air in the outward shockwave flattens anything not made of solid rock, as the shockwave races out faster than the speed of sound, and the sky fills with fire, smoke, ash, and deadly poison gases. Great destruction is wrought, and permanent, major environmental changes are brought, all because an overload of internal pressure found a little crack to push hard against. Once the little crack has been forced open, and becomes a raging torrent of molten rock, it can never be completely healed, or fully closed, again. It is always a weak spot, after that.

Now, picture that the entire Universe has a type of structural integrity which it is impossible for us to perceive, because the scale of the framework is far too vast for us to see, or to chart precisely. To our senses, or perception, space is rather empty, and has no viscosity at all, being just empty vacuum. That is a valid viewpoint, if the viscosity one is considering is only physical in nature, such as thick oil, or maybe honey.

There is another type of density which saturates the entire Universe, and that is the overall Universal gravitational field.

That structure, like any other physical structure, even though it is comprised of lines of force, instead of actual liquid or gaseous matter, has irregularities, or faults, scattered all throughout its' whole span. Some of the irregularities were from the wrinkles in the expansion patterns from the blast of the Big Bang. Some have developed over time from other cosmic events, such as the formation and initial collapse of large black holes, in the middle age of the Universe, while the structure was still in the formation stages, during the mid-expansion era.

(This reminds us of just how critical a role black holes play in the formation of galaxies, and also, new matter, as new elements are fused into existence, every time a star becomes nova, and black holes tend to cause a whole lot of that sort of chaos, out in the wilder zones of the sky.)

Why are the sky-faults important? Because they are the real-world "wormholes" that bad sci-fi writers have been misrepresenting, and misusing, just to make a hack story for a weekly episode in a series. Since they are real, and they do exist, they are the channels which allow the night sky version of over-pressurized sky-magma to vent, instead of splitting, not the planet, but the local space/time structure into pieces. The pressure must release, and it finds a pathway. The faults are not neat little tubes, as seen on TV. They are raw, ragged rips in the gravitational field, light-years wide, and are tears in the space/time framework, but because they follow along fault lines, they do not shatter the structure of the space/time matrix. (There is no sense of speeding along a tunnel. The transition is instant, and extraordinarily violent and explosive.)

The faults are normally closed enough to prevent any transfer of matter or even energy between remote points. Only when a sufficient level of internal pressure is achieved, will a rip in the fabric of space/time be opened. The required energy levels are only generated in the cores of large black holes.

All of that pent-up raw energy has to go somewhere. Even though the gravitational field of the black hole keeps the energy from escaping through normal space/time, the faults provide a possibility of pressure release. As nature abhors a vacuum, and always tries to fill it, and water seeks its' own level, so internal extreme pressure in anything seeks to vent, and to equalize pressure with the surrounding environment. Differences in heat also try to achieve balance. Hot things get colder, until they match the surroundings. Things with too much pressure usually explode, unless they are in an explosion-proof locked box. Therefore, when the cores of the black holes reach a certain critical level of strain, the fault is ripped wide open, and the energy from the core of the black hole is vented out into another time and space.

We cannot observe this process, since the rip is forced deep in the center of the large black hole, and we cannot ever see directly what is happening in there. Is there some place where we can observe the output of the core of the black hole, at the point where it re-enters space/time again? What will it appear as, and what will be its' characteristics?

To spot the output, we must search for something that is composed of the overloaded raw energy that was last known to be present within the core of the black hole. The only known structures which can even begin to approximate such outrageous levels of explosive force are the large quasars and blazars. Seyfert galaxies are something different, and are not any form of quasars, or blazars, since two traits of Seyferts are very different. They emit much lower energy levels, and they are all found much too near the Earth, near the center of the Universe's expansion.

Please consider a moment how the pieces of the puzzle now fit together, and form a coherent picture of events and the resulting structures and objects. The black holes collapse, increase in mass, reach the critical threshold, whatever insanely high level of energy pressure that may be, and then rip open an already existent (though still unopened) fault line. Once the plasma enters the fault, it widens, and the raw energy is instantly shunted out to the outer edges of Universal expansion, at the leading edge of the outward wave of Creation. When we perceive the quasars later in time, here upon Earth, we are seeing their ancient light, and their present position has moved much further out, still traveling along the outward motion bias from the big Bang, although other, newer quasars still keep appearing even further out, but their newer light has not reached us here, yet. The implication, and indeed, the actual fact of Reality resulting from that is that the quasars, alone of all things in the observable Universe, appear in reverse order of their age! The younger, more explosively energetic ones are the ones which we are seeing farthest away, since they have been unnaturally moved further out in the Universe! (The youngest of the new quasars we will not likely see for billions of years, even if their light is already racing toward us from the even still further expanded edge of the Universe, where it really is, today.)

Within the last decade, scientists have discovered that the outward Universal expansion is still accelerating, and they have struggled to explain this. One explanation from Dr. Hugh Ross is that the total energy balance in the Universe is now greater than the total mass balance in the Universe, and so the outward bound energy is moving everything else caught up in the initial flow even faster, outwards.

Another possible factor is, strangely enough, the gravitational field from the Great Attractor. As the mass of the monster increases over time, the gravity field expands, and the tidal force also expands. Tidal force stretches things out lengthwise along the lines of flux in the gravity well, as the proximity of the nearer end of the object is pulled much harder than the further out end, and this may also account for a measure of why the outer reaches of the fabric of the Universe are still stretching out, further and faster. (The larger the gravity field, the less we will be able to sense it or measure it, since it is dispersed over too great an area for us to be able to clearly detect it.)

At any rate, the outward thrust of the energy from the cores of the black holes is probably enough to accelerate expansion of the existing Universal structure. As near as we can estimate, the levels of energy from the quasars may actually be, in some of the extreme cases, of an order of magnitude that allows for generation of new space and time, which were fabricated from the raw energy of the Big Bang.

At the very least the generation of new matter, from the ejected raw plasma out of the cores, is certainly occurring continually. The quasars have been called the greatest particle accelerators in the present Universe, and that is partly correct. The particle accelerators that are the cores of the monster black holes, which ripped open the faults in space/time, are even more powerful than the quasars they produced, since there is some energy loss incurred, just opening the fault, and holding it open.

When the energy is ejected, and travels outward in space, to the very edges of Reality, it not only accelerates the expansion, and creates at least new matter, and perhaps new space/time also, in relatively small bubbles around the quasars, but it also provides a stable release for the overload of energy concentration within the cores of the black holes. The balance of the Universal structure is restored, safely, by directing the blast outward, and hurling it far away from places like the Earth, where it would fry every living creature with a flesh body. The mass which is left behind, intact, when the matter is stripped down, upon entry into the event horizon of the black hole, is the solid, unmovable anchor point which forms a stable launch pad for the energy, so the landing zone of the blast is far, far away from its' origin. Also, since the energy transfer is occurring outside of normal space/time, the Newtonian equal-and-opposite reaction is not a factor. Any thrust effect is carried along with the energy out to the new location.

All right, so the fireball moves out to the extreme outer edge, and keeps moving outward, burning outrageously brightly. It keeps shining brightly from then on, as long as the fueling black hole continues to force out plasma to the new location.

Just where the new location exists, we already know. It is way, way out there at the fringes. The other aspect to consider is just "when" the new location exists. We know that the things which we see in our little telescopes are things from the ancient past. We perceive things as they were, before the delay of light travel over the distance. By rule of definition, the further out we see something, the more ancient it must be, since it must have formed long ago.

That's all very well and good, but what about the strange anomalies of the quasars? Once formed, and then relocated by the black hole, the resulting "white fountain" appears as if it might have formed very early in the Universe. That is not possible, since no huge black holes, that were massive enough, had had time enough to form, not in the first few hundred million years of the Universe. That would be utterly absurd. It would take several billion years from Big Bang, and would almost certainly require second or third generation galaxies like our own, to produce the ultra-monster black holes that produce the quasars. (The Great Attractor, whatever it actually may be, does not fit in with any of the rules about anything else we know about the Universe. I suspect that it writes its' own rules, sort of like the 800-pound gorilla, in cosmic terms.)

That strange twist leaves us with a real mind challenge, to try to understand the apparent contradiction that something which could not possibly have formed 12 billion years ago is, or at least perhaps, "was", 12 billion years ago, emitting vast torrents of light, from a region of the Universe so ancient, that stars and galaxies had only just begun to even condense and ignite, and nothing out there, except maybe the Great Attractor, was large enough to make a quasar, by any means! So, how did they get way out there, back in the ancient Universe?

Perhaps it is a phenomenon that when the core ejects the raw energy from itself, it sends it outward, to the very fringes of Reality, because it has to place it there. Maybe it cannot re-appear completely inside normal space/time. The outward thrust maybe a combined result from the outward movement flow still operating in the expansion wave, and the effects of a built-in resistance from the Universe, as designed and built by Almighty God, to allowing the energy to manifest within fully formed space/time. Maybe the concept would be similar unto the way bubbles rise in a glass of champagne. That would account for a lot of the mystery, as to why the quasars always seem to appear far more ancient, by position, than they actually may be. When they are transferred through space, they are also automatically moved back through time, since the structure is a composite of both time and space. Perhaps this is a real world application of time travel, but, as with the impossibility of any practical use by human bodies of a "wormhole", there can also never be any practical use by a human body of a "time machine", since to use it would move the traveler out to the edges of the Universe, whether he wanted to go there, or not. (Also, it would by definition be a one-way journey, in both time and space.)

Therefore, you can see that our good Lord does things in a logical and comprehensible manner, even if it takes us a few thousand years to understand it. I still do not understand it all, but our good Lord does. I was just commanded to sit down and write the things which were shown unto me, in my strange dreams. I hope that I got it right, or at least, close, and that with the guidance of the Lord Holy Spirit, you will be able to continue your own exploration of these mysteries. I am left with more questions than ever, but I also have been given a couple of the answers which I was seeking.

All right, so now you will have to have strange dreams yourself, about the nature of God's Creation. I wish you many happy, although sleepless nights, up late, wrestling with the mighty concepts, which our good Lord has just allowed me to write down for you. May your journey of discovery be fruitful, and may you enjoy the quest to understand, almost as much as I have enjoyed my own!

As long as you seek King Jesus Christ, and are always hungry for the knowledge of truth, may you be blessed by the

Father, the Savior, and the Holy Spirit, in your search.

WAR COUNCIL

The people gathered together this day had all known each other for a very long, long time. Some had been friends only for a few centuries, but many had known and fought beside each other for thousands of years, in many different wars. A few even had friendships that stretched all the way back to the Beginning. King Jesus Christ had known all of the cherubs since the foundation of Reality, and also all of the seraphs, and the rest of the angels very shortly thereafter. The men that were also present at that meeting had each been known by the Lord since before the world began, but they had not lived, until He had actually created them.

Men and angels were not the only special creatures represented there. There were the founding, original members of some of the major animal species that had shared in the long war against evil, and had often helped men to survive, and even thrive, and increase, where they would have otherwise certainly been easy pickings for the devil, if not for the help provided by the good Lord, through our patient animal friends.

The Cherub of Space, Michael, was there, also in his military role as Commanding General of the Army of Heaven. The General of the Angels, Tzedek-el, was also present, listening eagerly for battle plans, hot to be on to the fight. That tough guy had been chomping at the bit for a long time, to finally get some full-power shots at the demons which were troubling the little brothers and sisters of King Jesus. Also in attendance was the Cherub of Time, Gabriel, ready to be told the final details of his personal part in the upcoming, overwhelming, sterilizing assault by the Army of Heaven against the enemy, and all of its' works, and all of the evil, rebellious people which had sided with the devil, against King Jesus. (The mightiest of all of the cherubs, Eden-el, the Cherub of Energy, was still on duty at the entrance to the Garden of Eden, preventing anyone but King Jesus from entering, until his orders were changed, just like he had been doing nonstop, since the time of the Garden, in the Beginning. He would join in the final assault, later, but was still on station, right now.)

All seven of the deadly war-seraphs were there, as well. Those ferocious destroyers could each one wipe out a nation, or a continent, in a matter of minutes, single-handedly. Each one of them was destined for an individual, especially tough target, the moment when the attack was launched. They would receive their target list today, just like everyone else here. The information had been kept sealed since before the world began, but King Jesus was about to reveal each person's general and specific assignments, and precisely how the timing would be keyed, and synchronized.

The amount of raw firepower which would be applied by the Army of Heaven would be the forever-ultimate example of overkill. Only about a half of the Army would actually be needed, even in the most extreme battle conditions, and victory was already assured, anyway, because it had already been recorded as such, in the Prophecies of King Jesus Christ, which cannot be broken.

These angels were not restricted to the use of only swords and shields. The modern Army of Heaven uses lasers, and both rifles and pistols, and machine guns, and hand-held cannons, and missile launchers, and rocket launchers, and grenades, and tomahawks, and throwing knives. When the troops in the Army are about 12 feet tall, and weigh over a thousand pounds, each, and all of it is rock-solid muscle, it is not a challenge to carry extremely large, heavy-firepower type weapons. If no other weapon is handy, any angel of Heaven can just pick up the nearest car or pickup truck, and throw it faster than sound waves at the enemy. (The muscle is not just flesh muscle. It is spirit-muscle, and it is thousands of times stronger, and does not tire in battle.) These fancy new weapons would be the envy of any Earthly army, but are way too powerful to give to men. Of course, they work against all flesh, but they also are designed to hurt and wound demons, too. (One of the unique and special weapons was similar in concept to a thing used by some police departments upon Earth. Included in the arsenal were launcher-guns that fired a type of net, which shot out, and entangled an enemy, and dropped him instantly to the ground, where he could be rounded up later, after the battle was over. The nets were not fabric, but were woven from modified gravitational fields, which kept even a demon from escaping.)

Every person at this council meeting had a lot of experience fighting against the enemy, and every one of them had either proven to be 100% loyal, such as with all of the good spirits of Heaven, or had been forgiven and restored, such as with all of the humans present, except for King Jesus. (King Jesus is the One which restores everyone else!) Once the forgiven humans had passed through death, they could not die any more, and neither could they sin any more, forever. Sin equals death, and no forgiven and resurrected human could ever die again, so he could never sin again, either. It was hard-wired into people after resurrection that they could never even want to sin again, for eternity. (They still have free will, completely, but they will never want to sin. It's like they could eat anything in the world, literally, but there are certain things in this dirty world which no sane person would ever want to eat. It will be like that, in a similar manner.)

The animals waited respectfully, mingled in among all of the men present. All of the animal commanders were males, as were all of the humans, and all of the Heavenly spirits there, also.

Women are wonderful experts, at changing houses into homes, and also, when loving, encouraging, protecting, teaching, feeding, and continually correcting children, pets, and their husbands.

Men are designed for war. We automatically know how to fight, and we automatically know how to kill. We automatically know that in some cases, words will not do, and only deadly force will solve the problem, justly. We understand that if you only wound evil, it will come back again later, and bring more evil helpers along with it.

Wolves know how to hunt. Men know all about war. So do the cherubs, the seraphs, and the angels. So does King Jesus Christ, the Holy Son of God.

King Jesus waited until all of them had finished flying, walking, galloping, hopping, or bouncing into the Command Center. The cherubs and the seraphs had shown up there by suddenly materializing right there, perfectly positioned where they would stand for the strategy session, fully ready to go, into total warfare, at any split second. Men had been designed for the capacity for warfare, and the ability to learn the skills of it, and become deadly at it, but the cherubs, the seraphs, and the angels were created knowing more than any human except King Jesus about combat and conflict. In a sense, they had been designed and built, from the start, although not just for these final battles, with these final battles in mind, and they were supernaturally equipped for unstoppable victory. The designs had proven unbeatable. None of the good spirits of Heaven had ever lost even an arm-wrestling match against any evil spirit. They could not lose, even though some times the fight was exhausting, and wounds could indeed be incurred, but would heal later.

None of the spirits, either good or bad, had ever yet been killed. That part was reserved for King Jesus Christ to accomplish, against the evil spirits, in the Lake of Fire.

As the last members of the military High Command of Heaven settled into their places, King Jesus looked all across the assembly of about 100 folks, of every kind and species that had helped the sons and daughters of Adam and Eve to outrun, outfight, outwit, outmaneuver, and outlast even the most crazy, extreme, and vicious assaults and persecutions of evil, ever since the Garden. These noble creatures, and their descendants and cousins, had been the witnesses, giving testimony in blood, with teeth, claws, swords, arrows, slings, and spears.

Sometimes the blood had been that of enemy agents. Sometimes, the blood had been their own. They had each paid whatever price was required of them, to accomplish their personal mission, as assigned by King Jesus.

King Jesus cleared his throat a bit, just to focus their attention, and began, "Today is the final planning and strategy session which we will need, before we begin the final assault. The plans will not fail. Each of you will not fail. You all have My Word on it! Now, as to specifics, each of you has a predestined role, and a pre-designated target, or list of targets. Go down the lists of targets in order, since I have them set in priority sequence. The timing in certain operations is absolutely critical, and I will help to co-ordinate those items, as will Gabriel, with each of the team leaders involved in a split-second type operation, especially the combined ops with more than one department in play at a time."

King Jesus paused a moment, and smiled a quiet, wistful smile, as He sighed a bit, and then said, "I truly do wish it had not come down to this. I tried to warn them, all of you tried to warn them, even the planet Earth (and the seas), and the Sun, the moon, and the stars tried also to warn them. Now, we cannot wait any longer. It is time that we begin this last phase, since we will complete it on time, as Father has ordained, before the world began."

He resumed, "Some of the operations will take a few years, so that is why the whole picture has to be shown unto you at this time, although some of you will not actively launch your particular part of the assault until much later. Each of you will know, as soon as I have finished your personal update. Before we go any further, I need to bring everyone up to current situation, down upon the battlefield. Please, everybody relax your shoulder muscles, take three deep breaths, really slowly, and then look deep into My Eyes, and just keep looking there, no matter what else that I show you as well. You do it too, animals, and even you, cherubs. Everyone, do it now!"

As soon as He said that, all of them obediently did the three slow, deep breaths, and consciously made their shoulders and necks relax, and then locked their eyes into the infinitely deep, loving Eyes of King Jesus.

Suddenly, every one of them saw real-world, real-time events, all over the Earth. Their minds were flooded with the sights and sounds of things ranging from the ongoing struggle against the sub-human beast Assad in Syria, to the children forced into either becoming murdering, 9- and 10- year-old slave-mercenaries, or 9- or 10-year-old sex slaves, if they were girls, to heartless animal abuse, to back room deals, with politicians in every party trying to trade their votes and influence for dollars. They saw deliberate pollution, intentional addiction efforts by cigarette companies and prescription drug (or sorcery) companies, unjust taxation, outright extortion, murders, rapes, robberies, thefts, lies, evil intents in evil hearts, and difficulty staying humble and loving, even for the elect.

They saw divisions in the people of God. They saw fear rule over people, instead of faith. People were rewarded by the devil for evil and lies, but those who sought to bear witness to the truth were hated and hunted, for the sake of the Name of King Jesus Christ. Even though God had been extraordinarily good unto mankind, mankind did not give a hoot about God, or any of God's Ways, or Laws. People chose to glorify and honor the evil things in the world, instead of God. They wanted to worship the things which God had made, instead of the God

Who made them, and those things which they liked so much better than Him.

Bankers continued to lie, cheat, and steal their ways into retirement (in this life, but hell after this) and lawyers continued to play con-man with a license to deceive, and doctors continued to overcharge, instead of cure, and terrorists continued to try to do pointless destruction to innocent, honest citizens. People kept on trying to cover up their evil, instead of confess it, and repent of it, and so, they continued to be unable to prosper, and, even worse, instead of admitting that they were the source of their own misery, they blamed the truly faultless, good-hearted God!

They saw Putin in Russia, celebrating another election victory, despite huge ongoing street protests all over Russia. Putin had learned a sneaky trick from the U.S., and how they handled a street protest, and the difference that made, instead of the way Asad was failing to

handle street protests in Syria. The smart
thing to do was to let the masses
complain, and tell them what they wanted
to hear, and then, somehow sneak in a
way to go on and do whatever the tyrant
wished to do, anyway. The U.S. and
other western nations had been using that
trick, very successfully, ever since the
Viet Nam war.

Strangely enough, the election victory
would keep Putin in power for another
six years. That would last him right up
until just about the time of the return of
King Jesus Christ. Putin would be the last
Russian ruler, and his reign would last
until the end of the world!

Western reporters entirely misread a
streak of tears down one side of Putin's
face, as he smiled for the cameras upon
his victory announcement. He said later it
was just a sharp, cold wind that had hit
him in the eye, at that moment, and there
had been no emotion behind it. He was
right. He only had cold steel for a heart,

but he would one day prove that fact to the world, and then see what the western reporters said about that. Nobody, but nobody, called him a crybaby.

They watched Abdullah of Jordan, having strange dreams, visions, and even visitations, on a routine basis, from the devil in person, as he groomed Abdullah for the central role which he would soon play in the endgame to erase Israel. Putin was ruthless, and savage, but to look inside Abdullah's dark heart was a shock, even for the mighty ones of Heaven. In all their centuries of war, they had never seen any human heart more saturated and overflowing with self-centered pride, and radiating out determined, rebellious hatred for God. It made all of them want to vomit with disgust. Of course, all of them knew very clearly that this monster was the one called the "anti-Christ".

They saw the Chinese, continually plotting how to conquer everything else in the Universe, but the same was also true of Abdullah, and Putin. Assad and other deluded maniacs already thought that they owned the Universe, by birthright.

They saw the rising tide of the newly forming Muslim Confederacy, which included nearly thirty countries, but only had about a dozen major players. All of the whole confederacy of murderers pointed their bullets toward Israel, and began to move their tanks and planes and ships in that direction, also. They did not realize that the good Lord was drawing them closer to His home turf, so the good angels would not have to chase them down so far, when they came to round them up, bind them, and then throw them into the Lake of Fire.

The business of men and nations was not all that the good Lord chose to reveal to them. He also showed them many troubling things about nature, including problems with the atmosphere, the magnetosphere, which shields the Earth from solar flares, all of the oceans of the Earth (the hydrosphere), the Sun itself, the moon, Mercury, Venus, and Mars, as well. The entire inner Solar System was disturbed, extremely, and corrective measures would have to be applied, and some of the more severe cases had to be started immediately. Balance must be restored!

One of the most very distressing things was the monster volcano, Yellowstone. It was already straining at the leash, trying to explode, and demolish 85% of the U.S. contiguous 48 States, which destruction it could achieve, within a few hours. Alaska and Hawaii would not escape, because the Earthquakes and shockwaves generated by a Yellowstone explosion, would, at the least, induce incoming tidal waves against both Alaska and Hawaii. Their coastlines, and all of the population there, would not survive. Once the monster blew, it would effectively remove the U.S. from the world scene,

even if there were a few survivors, here
and there.

Suddenly, the information update was
over, and everyone was instantly right
back in the present, in the Command
Center, blinking their eyes, as if waking
from a nap, into bright light. Now, every
one of them knew precisely what level of
craziness the world had descended into,
and just how much lower it would
certainly go, if left unchecked. It was
right at the very tipping point of no
return. The good Lord had not
exaggerated one little bit, when He had
said that the time was indeed now, or
never.

After giving everybody a moment or
two to absorb all of that, He spoke again,
"All right, now you know all of the major
grisly details. A lot of things must be
done, quickly, to even keep the gate of
"salvation opportunity" open long
enough to allow the last names already
written in the Book of Life to be called

by the Holy Spirit, and to respond, and hear, and obey, and be saved. We will start some of the measures as soon as this Council concludes. Now, I want you each to look into My Eyes once again, and I will show you, every one of you, what his part will be, and when and how you will do it. Trust Me. I already have all of the details worked out, perfectly!"

He looked over all of them, making brief, but intense, warm contact with every person there, for a split second or two, and then He smiled, and said to them all, "I have found a strange thing today. It is actually very difficult for Me (Who's not ever at a loss for Words) to adequately express My Personal gratitude to each of you. You have served excellently, and very willingly done, too, and you have delighted My Heart with your loving loyalty. When this is over, I have a special promotion and reward in mind for each of you, something each individual person desires most.

Remember, I can see your hearts. I see your love and goodness in there."

Suddenly, He focused His Eyes upon a small brown and white furry fellow, way at the back of the great company of ultra-heroes. He laughed, and said, "Okay, I see in your fearless great heart, little Wolverine, that you have something in there which you are afraid to ask Me! Little friend, ask! I want everyone to hear the answer, too."

Obediently, the little ferocious snow monster raced all the way up to the foot of the Throne, by his strange little bouncing run, front legs at the same time as a pair, then back legs at the same time, as a pair. He halted uncertainly, then mustered up every scrap of his nearly unlimited courage, and said, as calmly as he could, trying not to let his voice shake, "Yes, Lord, I am very sorry to interrupt the matters of the great folks, especially at a time like this, but I keep wondering why You did it. Why did You arrange this entire rescue mission we are about to do and even go Yourself, to pay for the sins of mankind? Why not just scratch them, and start over?"

King Jesus stepped down carefully from His Throne, so as not to frighten the little wolverine. King Jesus was about the only human ever that could frighten a full grown wolverine. They do not scare very easily. (He put the fear of man upon the beasts to protect us all from the wolverines, so that they would not eat the entire human race!)

King Jesus reached down, picked up the 45-pound bundle of teeth, claws, and muscles, and smiled at him, and said, loud enough so that they all could hear, "I did it because I love them. I love all of you, but I made them especially in My image, and I told them in the Beginning that I would save them, one day. Now, I am going to keep My Word!"

King Jesus put down the wolverine, which bounded back to where he had been, and he resumed his seat between Wolf and Bear. All three of them had met, and played, and fought in years gone by, back early in the world, in all the territory around Yellowstone. The huge volcano was part of their personal home turf.

Wolf leaned down, and quietly whispered into Wolverine's ear, "I told you to ask!"

Wolverine somehow managed to smile a very toothy smile, as he softly growled back, "Yeah, yeah."

All attention once more focused intensely upon King Jesus, as He continued, "Now, I will flash-download each commander's personal battle strategy and schedule, straight into your memories, where it will remain crystal-clear, for continuous reference as needed, until this is over, in about 6 more years. If you have any questions about any part of it, no matter how insignificant it might seem to you, let Me know, right after the meeting. I will help, and explain further."

King Jesus looked over all of them again, and said, "Okay, ready? Look at Me again."

Suddenly, each of them could see the entire, specific part his division would play, and precisely where, and precisely when, down to the very tiniest correct detail. Each commander saw not only his own personal location and actions during the coming six years, all at once, he also could easily see all that was under his direct authority, for the coming battles and campaigns. Wolf could instantly see everything which he personally was going to do, and he could also see everything that each of the millions of wolves in the Mighty Wolf Pack of Heaven (of which Wolf was, of course, Alpha Male) was going to do, but in much more general terms. He could quickly focus his attention on any one wolf, or group of them, and sort of zoom in to view a lot more detail, the closer he focused. He could also zoom back out, even beyond the domain of his wolves, and see how he and Adam would be interacting, in the joint strikes which they would be conducting, along with large teams of other men and wolves. Each of the other commanders was experiencing the same precise phenomenon, since that is the Way which the good Lord had known that the information would be most accessible, and useful.

As each of the creatures was adapting to the new way of perceiving, and viewing things, they began to see the current real-time situation clearly again, but the other informational views remained available, in a sort of heads-up display manner, with a see-through transparency to either the real-time view, or the internal information view, whichever the person was most intensely needing. (The shift was engineered into it, by King Jesus, and it operated automatically.)

King Jesus spoke again, "Take a little while, and get used to it. It will work smoothly for you, after a few minutes of practice. If any of you have any trouble seeing the information this way, let Me know that as well, after the meeting, please. You might be curious as to how the views, even of the future, can be so precise, and perfect in every clear, microscopic detail. I know that you noticed the holographic, 3D, stereo-surround nature of the information feed. Remember, I already live in the future, as well as the present, and the past. What I have done is download into your minds My own future awareness of all that is going to happen, as pertains to each of you, and your divisions. Wolves and bears do not need to know everything about each other's movements and doings, unless they are performing a combined operation together. Then, they must each know."

"All right, thanks again to each of you, noble Warriors of Heaven! Go and get ready for each of your parts, and inspect your troops, and, if you need to, any special equipment or preparations which need work. Cherubs, seraphs, and angels, you each know what part you have, and you know which elements need to start today. Gabriel, as you know, I want you on station right now, so go stand on top of Yellowstone, and do not let the enemy, or anything else, disrupt the peace there, not until the precise moment when I command you to let it loose! All the rest of you, get ready: the Time is almost at hand! Until we launch the final assault, then, SHALOM!!!"

As the King said this, He leapt upon the mighty back of His Personal War Horse, Tzedek-Sus (which had once been the little gray donkey, which had carried Him into battle, in Jerusalem), and He sped off into remote parts of Heaven, to be about His final preparations for the Last Battle.

The rest of them all dispersed, and, since the presentation had been so perfectly clear, there was not a single one which did not understand. King Jesus Christ had seen this knowledge in their minds, just before He had departed, and so, He had not stayed to answer any more questions. He already knew that they did not have a single question left, unanswered, for now.

ABOUT THE AUTHOR

When a person stops a moment to ponder the majesty of God, and the goodness that He very generously gives all of us, it makes a wise person's heart want to give back something good, to God. We can start with our thanks, and continue with our obedience. Even so, sometimes, a person realizes just how truly blessed he has been, all of his life, even when in pain, or sorrow, or troubles. Then, the person wants to try to do something special to honor Almighty God, and to help other people to understand just how very wonderful God really is, to us all. After all, are we not just animated mud-balls, with an electric spark or two in our heads, and the wind of life in our lungs?

These books were the best way I could find, to tell people about how good God really is. I tried to get all, and I do mean all, of the facts straight. Please recall that I am human, and might have made a mistake or two, but, ever since book 1, no one has yet been able to disprove a single one of these ideas or concepts. Some folks disagree, of course, but no one has yet proven any of it to be incorrect.

I hope you enjoy the books. I fought a war, to write them.

BACK JACKET TEXT

How do the pieces of the puzzle called Creation fit together? How does the unseen part of Reality match up and parallel the things we see in telescopes?
Even more important, does God have any mercy in His heart for us? (That question becomes more urgent, when you're facing more trouble.)
Here are clues, to seek further.

www.ingramcontent.com/pod-product-compliance
Lightning Source LLC
Chambersburg PA
CBHW070308030726
47505CB00004B/947